I0663037

# THE GUNSMITH

## 440

## Lost Man

Books by J.R. Roberts
(Robert J. Randisi)

*The Gunsmith* series

*The Lady Gunsmith* series

*Angel Eyes* series

*Tracker* series

*Mountain Jack Pike* series

COMING SOON!

**The Gunsmith**
441 - Aces & Queens

**For more information visit:**
www.speakingvolumes.us

# THE GUNSMITH

## 440

## Lost Man

J.R. Roberts

SPEAKING VOLUMES, LLC
NAPLES, FLORIDA
2018

Lost Man

ISBN 978-1-62815-931-8

# Chapter One

Clint Adams hadn't seen anyone for hours, riding across the Missouri plains, heading toward the town of Carthage. But suddenly, ahead of him, appeared a group of men who, more than anything else, resembled a posse.

As he approached them the man at the head of the group waved him down.

Clint reined in his Darley Arabian in front of the men, who all stared at him. There were at least a dozen of them and they were all armed.

"Posse?" he asked, despite the fact that there wasn't a badge in sight.

"Not exactly," the lead man said, "but we are lookin' for a man. Have you seen anybody in the area on foot?"

"Not on foot, not on horseback," Clint said. "Nobody. I was wondering why the area was so deserted, until I saw you fellas."

"Not so deserted," the man said, "but a bunch of us are out lookin' for a missing man."

"Missing?"

"He wandered off," the man said. "His family's kinda worried. He's not, ya know—" the man rapped his head, "—all there."

"Ah, I get it."

"We're hopin' to find him before he hurts himself," the man went on. "We got other groups out lookin', includin' the chief of police."

"Well, if I see him, who do I talk to?" Clint asked.

"My name's Hardesty," the man said. "The chief of police is Collins."

"And this fellas name?"

"Horton," the man said, "Ted Horton. The Horton family is one of the richest in Carthage."

"That explains the all-out search," Clint said. He wondered, if the missing man was poor, if there'd be as many men out looking.

"Well," Clint said, "I happen to be heading for Carthage, so if I see anything I'll pass the word."

"Much obliged," Hardesty said.

"We better keep ridin'," Hardesty said to the others.

He waited until they had all continued past him, then asked Clint, "By the way, what's your name?"

"Clint Adams," he said and then, without waiting to see if Hardesty recognized the name, he kicked his heels in Eclipse's side and headed for Carthage.

***

Carthage was a growing town, especially since the railroad had come. Nearby lead and limestone quarries had also done their part to increase the town's fortunes. As Clint rode down the main street he saw the kinds of stores you would see in most towns, in addition to a large foundry, a furniture factory, woolen and grain mills, Wells, Fargo station. Many restaurants and saloons. There were also plenty of hotels and livery stables for him to choose from. He also saw both a sheriff's office, and a new police station.

But for such a growing town, the streets were bare, quite a few of the shops had closed early. He assumed many of the townspeople were involved in the search for the missing man.

Luckily he found both a livery and a hotel that were still doing business.

"Why the hell would I be out lookin' for a Horton?" the liveryman asked. "I got a business to run."

"You don't like the Hortons?"

The 50ish, burly man glared at him and replied, "I just said I got a business to run. What's that gotta do with likin' or not likin' somebody. You wanna put your horse up here or not?"

"I do," Clint said, and stopped talking.

He decided not to even ask the desk clerk the same question. He simply signed in at the Westchester Hotel and accepted his key.

He got a room off the main street, as requested, and decided that the only person he knew he could ask questions of who wouldn't get insulted or angry was a bartender. It was their job to pour and talk.

He'd passed plenty of saloons on his way into town, and they all seemed to be open, so when he left the hotel he simply headed for the closest one. In addition to being curious, he needed a cold beer real bad to soothe his trail dust covered throat.

He entered the Arrowhead Saloon, found it as deserted as the streets. The bartender was standing at the bar, cleaning glasses—which was always a good sign. Either it was a clean place, or the man was looking for something to do to kill the boredom. There was only one other man in the place, and he was sitting at a back table with his head down, and a bottle of whiskey next to it.

"Pretty empty," Clint said, as he got to the bar.

"It'll fill up," the man said. "Whataya have?"

"Beer, and I hope it's cold."

"Like ice, friend," the bartender said, "like ice."

He was right. While it cleared Clint's throat, it nearly froze it.

"What's going on in town?" Clint asked. "Looks empty."

"Everybody's out lookin' for a lost man."

"Lost?"

"Lost, missing, whatever you wanna call it," the bartender said.

"I did run into some men outside of town," Clint said. "I thought it was a posse."

"The sheriff?"

"No, a fella named Hardesty."

"Ah," the bartender said, "Hardesty. He works for the Horton family."

"The family of the missing man?"

The bartender nodded.

"Foreman?"

"If it was a ranch, he'd be the foreman," the bartender said. "They call him their manager."

"And the men with him?"

"Volunteers."

Clint looked around at the empty interior of the saloon.

"So that's where your customers are?"

"Some of them."

"Why aren't you out looking?"

"I've got a business to run," the man said. "I ain't rich like the Hortons."

"Do you now the lost man?"

"I've seen him," the bartender said. "I don't know 'im."

"Could he have left on his own?" Clint asked.

"A runaway, you mean?"

Clint nodded.

The bartender shrugged.

"I don't know."

"Hardesty told me the man was . . . not right in the head," Clint said.

"I guess he should know," the barkeep said. "He's part of the family."

"So they figure he wandered away, not knowing what he's doing?"

The bartender shrugged.

"What if he was kidnapped?" Clint asked. "I mean, if the family's rich—"

"He's been gone since yesterday, and there ain't been a ransom note. Leastways, not that I know of. What's your interest anyway?"

It was Clint's turn to shrug.

"Just curious."

# Chapter Two

Clint took the bartender's advice when it came to eating somewhere. He left the saloon, walked down the street and stopped at a restaurant called THE TENDER CUT.

"Steak," he told the waiter, "with the works."

"Comin' up. Beer?"

"Definitely."

The waiter, a small man in his 60s, nodded and headed for the kitchen. There were a dozen tables in the place, but only one other was taken by a man eating a bowl of stew.

The waiter brought his steak dinner and beer at the same time.

"Always this busy?" Clint asked.

"What?" the waiter asked, then realized Clint was being sarcastic. "Oh, no, there's a missing man and folks are out lookin' for him."

"Missing? Or lost?"

"Honestly," the waiter said, "I don't know. We just heard yesterday that he wasn't home, and his family's lookin' for him. Folks turned out to volunteer to help."

"They like the fella that much?"

"I, uh, gotta go back to the kitchen" the waiter said and withdrew.

Clint heard laughing, looked over at the only other person in the place. The man was looking at him.

"What's funny?" Clint asked.

"Oh, sorry," the man said. "I wasn't eavesdropping, but I overheard—folks aren't out looking for Ted Horton because they like him. It's only because the family's rich. Nobody wants to get on their wrong side."

"What about you?"

"Me? I wouldn't be much help out there."

The man stood up, limped over to Clint's table and extended his hand. Like the waiter, he looked to be in his 60s.

"My name's Henry Skinner."

"Mr. Skinner," Clint said, shaking his hand, "I'm Clint Adams. I guess I interrupted your dinner."

"Ah, I'm finished," Skinner said. "I was just tryin' to decide what kind of pie to have for dessert."

"Partial to peach, myself."

"Well," Skinner said, "you got plenty of steak left there. Why don't I wait for you to finish, and then we can have some pie together? And we can talk."

"Sure," Clint said, "sounds good to me."

"I'll get my beer and join ya."

Skinner nursed his beer while Clint ate his steak and vegetables. At one point the waiter—Skinner called him Elmer—brought them each a fresh beer.

"Do you know Ted Horton?" Clint asked.

"I've seen him," Skinner said, "but I can't say I know 'im."

"What do you do in town, Mr. Skinner?"

"No, no," Skinner said, "you call me Hank. I got me a small shop in town, sellin' men's clothes. I used to be a travelin' drummer, but when I hurt my leg I had to give that up. So I settled here and opened my store. It ain't much, but if you need a new hat or a new shirt, I got it for ya."

"I might take you up on that," Clint said.

"What about you?" Skinner asked. "Any truth to your reputation?"

"Some," Clint said.

"I guess there's a little truth everywhere," Skinner commented.

"What about the Horton family?" Clint asked. "What's the truth there?"

"They own a lot of the town," Skinner said, "most of the businesses in the surrounding area. They pretty much support the town."

"Which explains why everybody's volunteering their services."

"Right."

"Except for a few."

"Well," Skinner said, "I can't, but I probably wouldn't if I could. Ownin' my own business means I don't need them."

"I heard that from the bartender in the Arrowhead. He's not out looking because he has a business to run."

"Yeah, that'd be Benji. He owns the place outright, don't owe the Hortons nothin'."

"So anybody who owes the Hortons their livelihood is out searching?"

"Pretty much."

"Does that include the police and the sheriff?"

"Well, it includes the police," Skinner said, "that is, the chief and his four officers."

"And the sheriff?"

"You say you were at Benji's?"

Clint nodded.

"Had a beer," he said.

"Was there a fella at a back table with his head down?"

"As a matter of fact, there was."

Skinner nodded.

"That'd be the sheriff."

# Chapter Three

Clint thought Hank Skinner might be able to offer him some further insight into what was going on in Carthage, so he offered to buy the man a drink.

"I tell you what," Skinner said, "my shop is right down the street. I've got a good bottle of whiskey and, like I said, some good shirts. Why don't we go there? I'm closed, so nobody'll bother us."

Clint preferred beer to whiskey, but said, "Sure, why not?"

He paid for his meal and followed Skinner out to the boardwalk and up the street.

"Do you usually close this early?" Clint asked.

"I close when I want to eat, and then reopen, but today with everyone out searching, I thought I'd just stay closed," Skinner explained.

His shop was a small storefront squeezed in between 2 larger businesses. He used his key to open the door and waved at Clint that he should go first.

"That's okay," Clint said. "I don't like walking into dark rooms."

"Ah, I understand" Skinner said, "Allow me . . ." he entered first, and after a moment a lamp was lit illuminating the interior of the small store.

Clint entered and closed the door behind him. It was warm inside and smelled musty. He assumed that was from all the material, because shelves and wall space were taken up by shirts, jackets, trousers and hats.

"Let's go into the back room"

Skinner entered that room first and lit the lamp. As Clint entered he saw it was basically a storeroom, but there was also a desk, which indicated Skinner probably used it as an office.

The older man went to the desk, opened a drawer and came out with the bottle of whiskey and two glasses.

"So this Ted Horton, is he really unable to care for himself?" Clint asked. "Is that why so many folks are out looking for him?"

"I don't know him that well, like I said," Skinner replied. "But I know some people who do. It's amazing how so many people can have a different opinion of somebody."

"How do you mean?"

"I know one person who thinks he's simple minded. I know someone else who thinks he's a genius."

"How can that be?"

"They've each taken some of the things he says differently."

"And the family?" Clint asked. "What do they say? I mean, it was Hardesty who told me he wasn't right in the head. Have they had a doctor tell them that?"

"Doc Willis is the town physician," Skinner said. "He could probably tell you more if you're curious."

"That's one of my flaws," Clint said. "I'm too damn curious." He figured a doctor in this town would tell him only what the Horton family wanted him to.

They talked a while more about what Skinner used to sell on the road, how he hurt his leg—kicked by a horse—and what kind of shirt and hat he thought Clint ought to have.

By the time Clint left they had drank half the bottle of whiskey, and he had bought 3 new shirts, which Skinner insisted on wrapping in brown paper.

At the door Skinner asked him, "How long will you be in town?"

"I don't rightly know," Clint said. "I guess that's going to depend of my goddamned curiosity."

"Well," Skinner said, shaking Clint's hand, "if you stay around, I hope to see you again."

"I'd enjoy that," Clint said, and started walking away as Skinner closed then locked the door of his shop.

# Chapter Four

Clint went back to his hotel, took off his boots and gun, reclined on the bed. He knew he was lucky he had eaten a full meal or sharing half a bottle of good whiskey with Skinner would have put him to sleep.

He had a couple of books in his saddlebags but didn't feel like reading. And despite the whiskey, he didn't feel like sleeping. It was just too early.

He wondered if any of the searchers had come back in because it was getting dark. Since staying in his room wasn't an option, he pulled his boots on again, strapped on his gun, grabbed his hat and left the room.

\*\*\*

There were a few men and women in the lobby, talking, when he came down. They paused to look at the stranger. Clint assumed they had been out searching.

At that point a man entered the hotel from outside, wearing a police uniform. He walked directly to the front desk, looked at the registration book, and then at Clint.

"You folks clear out," he said to the others. "There's nothing for you to do here. You should continue looking."

"But he's a stranger," a woman said, pointing at Clint.

"That doesn't mean anything," the policeman said. "Now go."

The people reluctantly filed out, leaving Clint, the policeman and the desk clerk.

"You're Clint Adams, the Gunsmith?" the policeman asked.

"That's right," Clint said. "What's going on?"

"Some people heard there was a stranger in town, thought you might have something to do with Ted Horton missing."

"Who are you?" Clint asked.

"I'm Chief of Police Collins," the man said. He was tall, in his 50s, filled out his uniform like a man who kept himself in shape.

"How did you hear I was in town?"

"First from Hardesty. You ran into him outside of town. Then I talked to the bartender at the Arrowhead Saloon."

"Benji."

"Right. He told me you were in town. This is the second hotel I'm checking."

"Well," Clint said, "here I am. The townspeople think a stranger took Ted Horton?"

"What do you know about Ted?"

"Just what Hardesty told me, and Benji." He left Skinner out, for now.

"Mr. Adams," Collins said, "I'd like you to come back to the police station with me and have a talk."

"Are you done looking for Horton?" Clint asked.

"I might be, for tonight," Collins said, "but I've still got men out there looking, and most of the town."

"And you came back to talk to me?"

"Well," Collins said, "it isn't every day the Gunsmith comes riding into our town, is it?"

"I guess not," Clint said. "Okay, I don't see any harm in a little talk."

He allowed Chief Collins to lead him up the main street, lit by what looked to be electric lamps, to the police department building.

"They built this for us," Collins said, as he used a key to unlock the front door. "Going to build a larger one, too, now that we've got some electric lights."

"I heard you have four officers," Clint said, following him down a hall.

"For now," Collins said. "We'll be doubling that soon."

They entered an office. Apparently, the electricity in the street hadn't gotten inside the building yet, so he lit a lamp on his desk.

"Have a seat."

Clint sat across the desk from Collins.

"This goddamn search," Collins complained. "It's keeping me from my regular work."

"Like what?"

"Like interviewing men for the extra jobs," Collins said.

"Well then, I guess you better ask me whatever questions you want to ask me, and I'll let you get back to work."

Collins rubbed his face with both hands and sat back in his chair.

"What are you doing in Carthage, Mr. Adams?"

"Passing through."

"And asking questions about the Horton family?"

"Hardesty works for them, right?" Clint asked.

"That's right."

"Then I suppose the family was questioning me, first."

"Good point," Collins said. "So, if you're passing through how long do you plan to stay?"

"I don't know," Clint said. "I'm a bit curious. I might just stay until this fella gets found."

"Does that mean you want to help find him?"

"I think you've got enough people doing that," Clint said. "Seems to me they're going to be stepping all over each other before long."

"That's entirely possible," Collins said.

Clint slapped his hands on his thighs.

"That it?"

"That's it," Collins said. "I appreciate you coming over."

Clint stood.

"Are you going to pass the word that being a stranger in Carthage isn't a crime?"

Collins smiled.

"I'll put the word out," Collins said, "but given who you are you might attract more attention when you're not a stranger."

"I get your meaning," Clint said. "I'll try to keep a low profile."

"Do that," Collins said. "I'd appreciate it." He stood. "I'll walk you out."

When they got to the front door Chief Collins unlocked it and let Clint out.

"Oh, before I go," Clint said. "Should I check in with the sheriff in town?"

"If you like," Collins said, "but you'd probably have to do it every day."

"Why's that?"

"He wouldn't remember from one day to the next."

# Chapter Five

Out of curiosity—he couldn't get away from it no matter how hard he tried—Clint went to the Arrowhead Saloon.

"Back for more?" Benji, the bartender, asked.

"That's right."

"Return customers get the first one on the house," Benji said, setting a cold one in front of him.

"Does that include Chief Collins?" Clint asked.

"Ah, the chief didn't waste any time, I see," Benji said. "He's the law. I'm sorry if he—"

"I'm not here for an apology, Benji," Clint said. "You did what you had to do."

"Thanks for that," Benji said.

Clint looked around. The place was doing a better business, now that a lot of the searchers had given up because of the dark. At a back table, there was still a man with his head down.

"Is that still the sheriff?"

"It is."

"How does he keep his job?"

"The chief didn't tell you the sheriff's name?"

"No."

"It's Horton."

That surprised Clint.

"If he's family, why isn't he out looking?"

"Because he's there," Benji said. "Try to put him on a horse, he'd fall off and break his neck."

"But the family keeps him on as sheriff?"

Benji shrugged.

"What's Ted Horton to the sheriff?"

"His brother," Benji said. "The sheriff is Tim."

"So all these men here were out searching today?" Clint asked.

"Yeah," Benji said, "one or two of them were with Hardesty when you saw him."

"So no sign of Ted?"

Benji shook his head.

"None."

"And no ransom note?"

"Not that I heard. You think he was kidnapped?"

"I don't have any opinion," Clint said. "I just got to town. But I'm an outsider. I'm going to have some thoughts that nobody else will, because I'm not beholden to the family for anything."

Benji leaned his forearms on the bar.

"Seems to me the family oughtta be usin' you," he said.

"Why's that?"

"Like you said, you ain't beholden to them. You'll tell them the truth, and not just what they want to hear."

"Is that what the chief does?"

"If he wants to keep his job."

Clint finished his beer.

"I get it."

"You gonna stay around?" Benji asked. "You could just ride out and forget all about Carthage and the Horton family."

"I could do that," Clint said. "I guess I'll see how I feel when I get up in the morning."

"In that case," Benji said, "maybe I'll see you in here tomorrow night."

"Maybe you will, Benji," Clint said. "And I'll *buy* myself another beer."

Clint left, went to his hotel, and this time stayed in his room.

# Chapter Six

In the morning he could still taste the whiskey and beer from the night before. He washed his mouth out with water before pouring it from the pitcher into the basin to wash up. With progress encroaching more and more on Carthage he wondered when they would have indoor water closets?

The best way to get rid of the taste of the night before was with some breakfast, so he went down to the hotel's diningroom. He was halfway through his bacon-and-eggs when Chief Collins appeared at the doorway and walked over to his table.

"Coffee?" Clint asked.

"Don't mind if I do." The chief sat across from him, looking ragged. Clint poured him a cup from the pot he had ordered and pushed it over.

"What brings you here, Chief?" he asked.

Collins sipped some coffee before answering.

"I got an early morning summons from the Horton family," he said. "I went to see Cyrus."

"Is he the head of the family?"

Collins nodded.

"Ted's father."

"And Tim?" Clint added. "The sheriff?"

"Ah, you found out about that, eh?"

"From Benji."

"Good source of information, that Benji," Collins said. "Yep, Cyrus is father to Ted, Tim, Tom, and Eloise."

"Eloise?"

"They had more imagination when it came to naming a daughter."

"What did Cyrus want with you?" Clint asked.

"He didn't want me," Collins said. "He wants you."

"Me?"

Collins nodded.

"He heard you were in town," the chief said, "no doubt from his man Hardesty."

"Ah."

"He'd like to see you this morning," Collins said. "Wants me to bring you around."

"And what if I decided to go home this morning?"

"I think that curiosity of yours would have you stopping to see Cyrus first."

"You're probably right," Clint said. "Can I finish my breakfast?"

"Sure," Collins said. "I'll wait outside."

Clint was going to tell him to have another cup of coffee, but the chief was up and headed for the door.

\*\*\*

When Clint came out the front door of the hotel, Chief Collins was sitting in a chair.

"Ready to go?" he asked.

"How far?" Clint asked.

"The Horton home is outside of town," Collins said, standing. "We'll have to ride."

"I'll get my horse from the livery," Clint said.

"Meet me in front of the police station," Collins said.

They went their separate ways, came together again in front of the building with their horses.

"That's some animal," Collins said, looking at Eclipse.

"Not as young as he used to be," Clint said, stroking the Darley Arabian's neck, "but he gets the job done."

"Doesn't matter how old he is," the chief said, "that's the best looking horse I've ever seen."

The chief was riding what looked to be a 5 or 6 year old Morgan, the type that was used by a Calvary during the Civil War.

"Ready?" Collins asked.

"Let's go."

\*\*\*

It took them fifteen minutes of riding before Clint saw the house in the distance.

"Is that as big as it looks from here?" he asked.

"Bigger."

The chief was right. When they reached the house Clint thought it was easily the largest house he had ever seen—two floors, lots of windows. There was nothing around it that he could see, no outhouse or barns.

"How many rooms does this have?" he asked.

"Nobody knows," Collins said, dismounting, "except, maybe, the family."

"And how many of the family live here?"

"All of them. Tim and Tom with their wives, Ted, Eloise, Cyrus and his new wife, Elizabeth."

"New wife?"

"Brought her home last month. Much younger than him, just a little older than his oldest son."

"That sounds like it could lead to problems."

"Four women living in the same house?" Collins said. "You don't know the half of it. We can leave our horses here."

Clint followed Chief Collins up the front steps, and into the huge house.

# Chapter Seven

At first Clint was surprised when they entered the big house without knocking. But as they got inside he noticed some foot traffic in both directions. Men and women going this way and that, some greeting the chief, others ignoring them both.

"What's going on?" Clint asked.

"That's the way it is here," Collins said. "There are usually people going in and out, back and forth. Especially now that Ted's missing."

"But . . . who are all these people?" Clint asked.

"Some are family, some are neighbors helping with the search, and others are from town."

"Chief Collins!"

They both turned at the sound of the chief's name. Clint saw a lovely young woman in a blue dress, with long auburn hair, approaching them.

"Mrs. Horton," Collins said.

"What brings you here this morning, Chief?" she asked, looking at Clint.

"Your husband asked me to come by, and bring Clint Adams with me."

"Ah," she said, looking Clint up and down, "so this is the famed Gunsmith."

"Mr. Adams, this is Elizabeth Horton, Cyrus Horton's wife. Mrs. Horton, Clint Adams."

"I'm charmed," Elizabeth said.

"Where would your husband be at the moment, Mr. Horton?" the chief asked.

"He's in his office, Chief, still coordinating the search for Ted."

"Then I better get Mr. Adams in there," Collins said.

"Yes, he's probably waiting," Elizabeth said. "It was a pleasure to meet you, Mr. Adams."

"Mrs. Horton."

The chief led the way across the entry hall floor with Clint following, while Elizabeth stood there and watched with a smile on her face.

"So that's the young Mrs. Horton, eh?" Clint asked.

"That's her."

"She doesn't seem very upset about her step-son being among the missing," Clint commented.

"Well, it might have something to do with the fact that she doesn't know him very well," Collins said. "She's really just getting to know her new family."

"Under bad circumstances," Clint added.

"That's nobody's fault," Collins said, "except maybe Ted."

"Or anybody who had anything to do with him being missin'," Clint said.

"Believe me," Collins said, "that's something I'm considering."

They started down a hallway and had to step aside for a man who was storming their way angrily. As he went by, Clint saw the badge on his chest.

"Don't tell me, let me guess," he said to Chief Collins. "Sheriff Tim Horton?"

"Looks like he had some sort of run in with his old man," Chief Collins said. "Hopefully, Cyrus isn't in a bad mood as well."

They continued down the hall until they reached the open door of an office. Collins entered with Clint right behind him. There was a huge desk, some chairs, a few file cabinets and not much of anything else. The office was truly set up exclusively for business.

Standing behind the desk, talking to several men, was a tall, cadaverous looking man in his 60s. The surface of the desk was covered with maps.

Cyrus Horton spotted the chief, and then dismissed his men with a wave.

"Get back out there and find my son," he told them. "You have your marching orders."

"Yes, sir," they said, almost in unison, and left the room nodding at the chief as they went.

"Chief," Horton said. "Is that Mr. Adams?"

"It is, sir," Collins said. "Cyrus Horton meet Clint Adams."

Clint came forward and shook the older man's hand. The hand was thin, almost frail, but there was a lot of strength in the handshake.

"A pleasure," Clint said. "I'm sorry to hear about your son."

"I appreciate that," Cyrus said, "but right now he's just among the missing. I'm not assuming the worst. Would you have a seat, I'd like to talk to you."

"Sure."

Clint sat as Cyrus pulled over a chair and seated himself behind his desk. There was nothing fancy about the desk or the chair, they were functional.

Chief Collins stepped back and remained standing, his hands clasped in front of him.

# Chapter Eight

"My manager, Hardesty, told me he encountered you yesterday during his search."

"That's right," Clint said. "I thought he was leading a posse."

"Not quite," Cyrus Horton said, "although the law is well behind our search."

"Indeed," the chief said.

"Are you planning on staying in town long?" Horton asked.

"I'm not sure," Clint said. "I'm really not coming from anywhere or going anywhere, at the moment."

"That's good," Horton said. "Then perhaps you could be of some help to me."

"In what way?" Clint asked.

"Finding my son."

"You seem to have an entire town out doing that for you," Clint said.

"That's true," Horton said, "but they'll find him if he's simply wandered away, while not in his right mind."

"How often is he not in his right mind?" Clint asked.

"It comes and goes," Horton said.

"What's the cause of it?"

"A head injury, from his childhood," Horton said. "We've had to watch him carefully since then."

"So what happened this time?"

"It's my fault," Cyrus said. "I'm afraid I've been occupied with my new wife. Ted wasn't happy about my bringing her home. They . . . haven't been getting along. If he wandered away, it's because I wasn't watching him."

"And if he didn't wander away?"

"Then he was taken," Horton said.

"Mr. Horton—" Collins started.

"No, it's true," Horton said, raising a hand to silence the chief. "You don't become as successful as I without making enemies."

"And you think one of your enemies might have taken him?" Clint asked.

"It's possible."

"So you haven't heard anything," Clint said. "No ransom demands?"

"No, none," Horton said. "Yet."

"Mr. Horton," Collins said. "My men and I can pursue this possibility—"

"Your men are otherwise occupied, Chief," Cyrus said. "As are you."

"Then what would you have me do?" Collins asked.

"Continue your search," Horton said, "and leave me to talk to Mr. Adams. He can find his way back to town."

"Adams?" Collins said.

"It's okay. I can find my way."

"Then I'll go back to work."

The chief turned and left the room.

"And now we'll do business," Horton said. "How much do you want?"

"To do what, exactly?" Clint asked.

"Find out if my son was taken," Horton said. "And if so, who took him. And finally, where he is."

"You need a detective for that," Clint said. "A Pinkerton, perhaps, or someone I know—"

"There's no time for me to bring someone in," Horton said. "By the time they get here, it'll all be over."

"What do you expect me to do?"

"You're a stranger here," Horton said. "You have no preconceived notion about the people, about my family. You'll look into every possibility, without fear of offending anyone."

"Even you?"

"I don't care," Horton said. "I want my son found."

"How old is he?" Clint asked.

"Twenty-two."

"Is he your youngest?"

"Yes."

"How do his brothers feel about him?"

"They love him."

"Even Sherriff Tim? I saw him storming out of here."

Horton hesitated, then said, "Well, at least you get right down to it. Yes, Tim and I had a . . . falling out. He's not doing much to help find his brother. But it's not because he doesn't love him. It's because he's useless."

"Then why let him wear a badge?"

"I thought the badge might change him," Horton said. "Give him some sense of . . . purpose. It hasn't."

"Why doesn't he work for you?"

"He has no business sense."

"And what about Tom. He's your oldest?"

"Yes, he *does* work for me. He has good business sense. He'll take over when I'm gone."

"Where is he now?"

"Out searching."

"And your daughter? Eloise?"

"She loves Ted and is worried about him."

"Is she older than him?"

"Yes, by two years."

"She has no husband?"

"No. I'm afraid she's on her way to becoming an old maid."

"And what about Tim and Tom's wives?"

"Tim's wife is as useless as he is," Horton said. "Tom's is a gem."

"Tell me about Hardesty."

"He's been with me for years, like one of the family. He and Tom are thirty, the same age."

"How does he feel about Ted?"

"He loves him like a brother."

"Really?"

"Yes."

"How about—"

"You're asking a lot of questions," Horton said. "Does this mean you're going to help us?"

"It means I'm curious," Clint said. "There seems to be a lot going on here. And since I'd have a free hand when it comes to finding out about it all . . . then, yes, I'll help."

"I'll pay you handsomely," Horton said. "Whatever you want."

"That can come later."

"Really?" Horton asked. "You don't want to set your fee now?"

"It's not necessary. But you should know one thing."

"What's that?"

"My gun is not for hire," Clint said. "If your son was taken, and I find out who did, it won't kill them for you."

"That's fine," Horton said. "I just want him back safely."

"Where's the last place anyone saw Ted?"

"In his room."

"I'll want to see that."

Horton frowned.

"What do you expect to find?" he asked. "He's out there, somewhere."

Clint stood.

"There's one more thing you should know, Mr. Horton."

"What's that?"

"I'll do this my way, no interference."

"All right yes, of course. I'll take you to his room."

"Who was the last one to see him there?"

"Eloise."

"Then I'd like her to be the one to show it to me."

Horton frowned again.

"Have you done this sort of thing before. You seem to have definite ideas."

"Let's say one of my closest friends is a detective," Clint said, "and I've learned some things from him."

"That sounds like good news," Horton said. "Come on, I'll take you Eloise."

# Chapter Nine

Horton walked Clint out of his office, back down the hall to the front of the house, where the activity was. As they reached that area Clint saw that Horton's wife, Elizabeth, was still there, talking to another woman.

"Oh, good, darling" he said, "Did you meet Mr. Adams when he came in?"

"I did, dear," she said. She looked at the other older woman. "That's all, Mary."

"Yes, Ma'am."

"Mary is our cook," Elizabeth told Clint, as the woman walked away.

"Darling," Horton said, "Mr. Adams has agreed to help us find Ted. He wants to see his room, and he wants Eloise to show it to him. Do you know where she is?"

"I did," she said, "and I'll be happy to take him to her. You've got so many other things to do."

"There you are," Horton said to Clint. "Elizabeth will take you to Eloise."

"Fine," Clint said.

"Please, stop in and see me before you leave."

"I will."

Horton went back to his office.

"Eloise happens to be in her room," Elizabeth said. "I'll take you up."

"Thank you."

She slid her arm through his and started up the stairs with him.

"So tell me," she said, "what exactly are you going to do that nobody else can for the family?"

"Your husband feels if his son was taken, I'll find out, even if I have to ruffle a few feathers. He doesn't think the local law can or would do that."

"Well," she said, "the sheriff certainly wouldn't."

"Do you mind if I ask you a few questions?" Clint asked.

"Not at all."

They reached the top of the stairs and stopped.

"Where do you think Ted is?"

She waved her arm and said, "Out there, somewhere."

"How do you get along with your husband's children?"

"Not well," Elizabeth answered, "but I'm working on it."

"What about Eloise?" he asked. "Is it harder or easier with a girl?"

"It's been hard," she said, "but you'll see. Come this way."

She led him down a hall lined with doors, reached one that was closed, and knocked.

The girl who opened it did so with a storm cloud over her pretty head. She was blonde, and rather than being frail and thin like her father, she was firm bodied and obviously strong.

"Whatayou want?" she demanded of her stepmother.

"Eloise," she said, "this is Clint Adams. He's agreed to help the family find out if Ted wandered away, or was taken. Your father would like you to help him."

"Fine," the girl said. "He can come in. You can go away."

Elizabeth looked at Clint and said, "I'm sure Eloise will look after you. Excuse me."

Elizabeth went back down the hall as Clint stepped into the younger girl's room.

"What does my father think you can do?" she asked, closing the door. The room was very stark and neat.

"Find out if someone took your brother, or if he just wandered away. What do you think?"

"Honestly?" she said. "I think Ted got tired of the way he's treated here. I think he left."

"On his own?"

"Yes."

"I thought he couldn't take care of himself."

"That's what everybody tells him," she said, "but he doesn't believe it, and neither do I."

"Interesting," Clint said. "It's the first time I've heard that."

"So what does my father want me to do?"

"I want to see Ted's room." Clint said. "He said you'd show it to me."

"That's no problem," she said. "It's right down the hall."

She was wearing a simple green dress as she walked barefoot to the door and opened it again.

"Follow me," she said.

She led him down the hall to another room where the door was closed, opened it and ushered him in.

"This is Ted's room."

It was a mess. There were clothes strewn all about the floor and the unmade bed, a dresser drawer was open with articles of clothing hanging from it.

"Is it always like this?" Clint asked. "Or was the room searched."

"It's always like this," she said. "What would anyone have searched for?"

"Well," Clint said, "if he left on his own, maybe there's something here to tell us where he went."

"Like what?" she asked.

"I'm not sure," he said. "I'll probably know when I find it."

"Go ahead and search then," she said. "If you need anything else I'll be in my room."

"Okay," he said. "I shouldn't be too long."

She left, and he did a thorough search of the messy room. But it was all for naught. He didn't find any letters that might indicate where the young man went, and there was no way he could tell if any clothes had been packed.

He didn't find any guns. If Cyrus considered his son not right in the head, he probably didn't let Ted have any guns.

Clint walked to the doorway, took one last look around the room, then headed back up the hall to Eloise's room. The door was closed again, so he knocked.

"Is that you, Adams?" she asked.

"Yes, it's me."

"Come on in, then."

He opened the door, started in, but stopped short when he saw her standing there, naked.

"Well," she said, "come in and shut the door before somebody else walks by!"

Hurriedly, he shut the door, then turned to look at her again.

"We don't have all day," she said. "Get undressed— unless you don't want to fuck me."

# Chapter Ten

After a moment Clint was able to find his voice.

"I'm just a little surprised."

"Don't be," she said. "I'm sure this happens to you all the time. You have a certain reputation, you know, and I don't mean with a gun. Now come on."

The gunbelt came first, as usual, set down within easy reach. After that he got rid of the rest in no time and stood there as naked as she.

"My God," she said, staring at his penis.

"How do you want to do this?" he asked.

"Wait," she said, "give me a minute."

She walked to him, dropped to her knees, ran her hands up and down the backs of his legs while his hard cock was right there in front of her face. She pressed her cheek to it, then brought her hands around to grasp it at the base with one while she cupped his sack with the other. She then slowly took his penis into her mouth, and started sucking him wetly.

Clint didn't think he had the time to submit to this young woman's whims—especially not in her father's house. He leaned over, put his hands beneath her arms and hauled her off his cock and to her feet.

"We don't have time for this, Eloise," he said.

As solid a woman as she was, he lifted her and deposited her on the bed. Then he spread her legs, knelt between them and drove his hard cock into her soaking wet pussy.

"Oh, yesssss . . ." she hissed.

"We have to do this quietly," he told her, driving into her.

She laughed and replied, "It's a big house. I don't care who hears me. But come on, just fuck me, hard and fast. I already know we'll be doing this again somewhere else, and soon."

So he gave her what she wanted, slamming into her again and again, as fast and as hard as he could. She began to move her hips in unison with his, so that they were coming together with loud, wet, flesh-slapping sounds.

In spite of what she said about not caring, she turned and buried her face in her pillow every time she felt the urge to cry out. And when he felt his legs and thighs begin to tremble, he turned her over so that her face was buried in the pillow. The sight of her ass as he plowed into her a few more times brought him to his climax, and he pressed himself deep inside her as he ejaculated, causing a muffled scream to escape from her . . .

As he dressed she watched, still naked on the bed.

"You know," she said, breathlessly, "if Ted wasn't missing I wouldn't be letting you leave this room for hours."

"If your brother wasn't missing," he said, "I wouldn't want to leave this room for days."

She laughed.

"Does anybody in your family know this side of you?" he asked.

"Are you crazy?" she asked. "They think I'm an old maid virgin."

"How old are you?"

"Twenty-four, and my father expected me to be married years ago." She rolled onto her back and stretched. "I'm afraid I'm a great disappointment to him."

"Well," Clint said, "not to me."

She laughed, rolled over onto her stomach and looked at him again.

"A piece of advice before you go," she said. "Watch out for my dear step-mother."

"Why?"

"If you're not careful," Eloise said, "she'll have you in her bed, too."

"Not today," he said. "I'm afraid I'm a little worn out."

"I don't think so," Eloise said. "I think you can go and go. And I'm going to prove it—after you bring my brother back."

"Eloise—"

"Call me Lisa," she said. "I prefer it."

"Lisa," he said, "if your brother went off by himself, do you have any idea where he'd go?"

"If Ted left on his own," she said, "he's far away from here. You'll never find him. Your only hope is that someone did take him, or that he lost his head, wandered off, and will come to his senses soon."

"Thanks for your help."

He walked to the door.

"Thanks for yours," she said. "I haven't felt this relaxed in months."

# Chapter Eleven

Clint made his way down to the first floor. After spending time with Horton's daughter in bed, he wasn't that anxious to talk with Cyrus Horton again.

When he reached the first floor and started for Horton's office, Elizabeth came from what he assumed was the livingroom and grinned at him.

"You look tuckered out, Mr. Adams," she said. "Why would that be, I wonder?"

"I searched Ted's room very thoroughly."

"Anything I can do for you?" she asked.

"Actually, I was on my way to see your husband."

"I'll take you," she said, and slid her arm into his. She was tall, slender, sweet smelling and very beautiful, especially when she smiled.

"Can I ask you a question?"

"Sure."

"Why here?"

She laughed, squeezed his arm.

"I thought you were going to ask me about Ted."

"I'm just curious," he said. "A beautiful woman like you—"

"Mr. Adams," she said. "I'm a married woman."

"I know that," he said. "I was just—oh, never mind."

"No, no, I'm teasing," she said. "I'll answer the question. I met Cyrus in St. Louis, figured out he was rich, and when he asked me to marry him, I said yes."

"After how long?"

"Two days."

"Huh."

"That was long enough."

"So you married him for his money?"

"Well, of course," she said. "But I didn't know about the family." She leaned against him. "A little more than I bargained for."

"So, will you be leaving?"

"Probably," she said, "but I'll wait until Cyrus finds out what happened to Ted. No sense adding to his woes, just now."

"You're very considerate."

She stopped walking.

"Cyrus' office is just up ahead."

"Why are you being so honest with me?"

She shrugged. "Why not? I'm going to be honest with Cyrus pretty soon."

She started back down the hall. "Looking forward to seeing you again, Clint . . . under better circumstances."

He continued on to Cyrus Horton's office.

When Elizabeth reentered the livingroom she saw Tom Horton there.

"Tom."

"What's going on, Elizabeth?" he asked. "Who was that man you were just with?"

"His name's Clint Adams," she said. "He's working for your father."

"The Gunsmith?" Tom asked. He was as tall as his father but carried about 40 more pounds. A fit looking man. "What's he doin' for Pa?"

"Looking for your brother."

"We've got plenty of people doing that," Tom said. "Why does he need him?"

"You'll have to ask Cyrus," Elizabeth said.

"What are you doing?"

Elizabeth turned and saw Cassie, Tom's wife, standing in the doorway, hands on hips. She was an angular looking woman who some men would find attractive. She was also 5 years older than Tom, who was 30.

"You've got your own husband to spend time with," Cassie said.

"Hey," Elizabeth said, "he's all yours. I was just leaving."

She walked past Cassie and out of the room.

"What were you doin' with her?" Cassie demanded.

"Just what you saw when you walked in," Tom said. "Talkin' to her."

"Yeah, well, I know you wanna do more than that." she said. "I see the way you look at her."

"You're crazy," he said. He started past her. "I've gotta go find Ted."

She grabbed his arm.

"She's your father's wife."

"I know that, Cass," he said. "Now let me go and do what I gotta do."

She released his arm and he continued out.

***

Clint stopped in the office doorway and knocked. Cyrus looked up from his desk.

"Mr. Adams," he said. "Did you get to Ted's room?"

"I did," Clint said. "Is it always that much of a mess?"

"I'm afraid so. He's not real good at picking up after himself."

"I'm going to leave now," Clint said, "but I'll need somebody to show me around, maybe answer some more question.

"Tom was just here," Cyrus said, getting up from behind his desk. "Let's go see if he's still in the house. He'd be the one for you to talk to."

They walked back up the hall together.

# Chapter Twelve

"Tom!"

The man stopped on his way to the front door and turned, Clint could see the resemblance.

"Pa, what is it?" he asked. "I've gotta get back out there—"

"This is Clint Adams," Cyrus said. "Mr. Adams, this is my son, Tom."

"Good to meet you." Clint stuck his hand out. Hesitantly, Tom shook it.

"Pa, he's the Gunsmith."

"I know that."

"Why is he here?"

"He was passing through town, and he's agreed to help us find Ted."

"How?" Tom asked. "Excuse me, Adams, but how do you expect to do what the whole town hasn't been able to do, yet?"

"By asking the right questions," Clint answered.

"Pa—"

"I want you to help him," Cyrus said. "Show him around, answer his questions, give him whatever he needs."

"Are you sure about this?"

"I am," Cyrus said. To Clint he said, "I'll see you when you have something to tell me."

"Right."

Cyrus put his hand on his son's shoulder.

"Cooperate with him, son," Cyrus said. "It's just another avenue to take."

"All right, Pa."

Cyrus turned and headed back to his office.

"What do you want to do first, Adams?" Tom asked.

"Well, we could start with you calling me Clint," he answered. "And second, show me Ted's horse."

"He'd be in the barn," Tom said. "I was headed there anyway."

They left the house and went down the stairs. Tom stopped to look at Eclipse.

"That's your horse?"

"It is."

"My God!"

"I'll walk him with us to the barn," Clint said, taking Eclipse's reins.

They started walking.

"Why are you back?" Clint asked. "I thought you were out looking."

"I came back for a fresh horse."

When they reached the stable they went inside and Tom pointed.

"That mustang is Ted's."

"Well now," Clint said, "if your brother had gone off on his own, why would his horse still be here?"

"Who says he went off on his own?"

Clint decided not to give Eloise away.

"Just a suggestion I heard."

"You been talkin' to my sister, haven't you?" Tom asked.

"Why? Is that what she says?"

"She claims he told her he was leavin'," Tom said. "He just didn't say when."

"Your sister Eloise, she get along with Ted?"

"They got along real good," Tom said.

"And you?"

"Ted's my little brother," Tom said, "that's how I treat him. Besides, I'm too busy helpin' my Pa run his businesses."

"And what about your sister?" Clint asked. "You get along with her?"

"She and my wife don't get along," Tom said, "and a man's got to stand up for his woman, right?"

"I suppose. What about your other brother, Tim?"

"Tim's out there lookin'," Tom said, "but he ain't gonna find shit. Him and his wife are just livin' off Pa."

"So the women in this family don't get along?" Clint asked.

"Not one bit," Tom said. "Eloise hates 'em all, Elizabeth's got no use for any of us, men or women. My wife Cassie don't like nobody. And Tim's wife, Wendy, well, she kinda likes everybody, if you know what I mean. Especially men."

Clint wondered what Tom would do if he ever found what he and Eloise were doing just a little while ago?

"And all this family lives in one house?"

"That's right," Tom said, "Pa's house. And he never let's any of us forget it."

Clint was starting to figure, if Ted left by himself, he knew why. But still, why do that and leave your horse? The presence of the mustang in the barn seemed to indicate otherwise.

Clint examined the mustang, anyway.

"A sound animal," he said.

"Nothin' in this barn looks sound next to your horse," Tom observed.

Clint ignored the compliment to Eclipse.

"Has Ted got any friends in town?"

"I don't rightly know the answer to that," Tom said.

Clint listened to the way Tom spoke and figured he must have had some natural smarts if his father thought he was business minded, because he didn't sound like a man who'd had a lot of formal education.

"Tell me about Hardesty."

"Will is my Pa's manager."

"Runs the businesses?"

"My Pa runs the businesses," Tom said. "We all work for him."

"How did Hardesty get along with Ted?"

"Will has worked for Pa 'bout ten years, and I don't think he said ten words to Ted in all that time."

"Who does Hardesty talk to? You?"

"He's got it in his head he's gonna marry my sister," Tom said.

"And what does your sister say to that?"

"About the only smart thing she ever said was that he was crazy."

"And what's your father say?"

"He's in favor of it," Tom said, "which is probably why she's against it."

They walked outside the barn, Tom leading a horse he had saddled earlier, a 5 year old roan.

"What did your brother Ted do, every day?"

"Nothin'."

"He must've done something."

"We got a swimmin' hole nearby," Tom said. "Sometimes he'd go there."

"To swim?"

"To see if any gals from town, or from here, were swimmin'," Tom said. "He'd watch 'em."

"Your wife? And Eloise?"

"Even his own sister," Tom said. "Ted would watch any naked woman from hidin', if he could."

"And your father's wife?"

"Her, too."

"And none of them ever caught him?"

Tom rubbed his jaw.

"Elizabeth figured out he was there, but that just meant she put on a show for him. Showed him everything she's got."

"How do you know that?"

Tom laughed.

"She bragged about it once."

"To you?"

Tom nodded.

"She ever tell your Pa?"

"I doubt it," Tom said. "I think if Pa knew Ted was watching her, he'd've tanned his hide."

"Did your father beat Ted?"

"When he needed it."

"But he's a grown man."

"He don't always act like one."

"What about the rest of you boys?" Clint asked.

"He wouldn't dare try it with me." Tom put his hands on his hips and puffed out his chest. "What do you wanna do now?"

# Lost Man

"Show me the swimming hole."

# Chapter Thirteen

Tom and Clint rode out to the swimming hole at a canter, with Tom slightly in the lead. Clint knew Eclipse could outrun Tom's roan any time, but he remained just behind him. He already knew Tom was the kind of man who needed to feel superior, and in charge. It was his self-defense against his old man.

They rode up to the swimming hole, which at the moment had no swimmers in it.

"This is it," Tom said.

Clint dismounted, started walking around, studying the ground.

"What are you lookin' for?" Tom asked.

"Any indication that somebody's been here recently," Clint said, "doing something other than swimming."

"Like what?"

"I don't know," Clint said. "If he left on his own, maybe he arranged to meet someone here."

"What for?"

"I'll know when I find them."

Tom fell silent, then, and watched as Clint walked around the area.

What Clint found were some tracks at the far end left by horses and boots.

"Tom!"

Tom dismounted and walked over.

"What is it?"

"Has anyone been searching here?"

"I don't know," Tom said. "I haven't, I don't think anybody from the house has. Maybe from town. Why?"

"Somebody was here, and recently," Clint said. "See these tracks? They rode in, then dismounted."

"And did what?"

"Stood here, talked."

"Don't forget, Ted's horse is in the barn."

"Right," Clint said, "so he would've had to walk here from the house."

"It's a few miles."

"What kind of shape is he in?"

"He's young," Tom said, "he could've walked it."

"Right. I'm going to look around some more, see if I can find any tracks leading here."

Tom went and stood with the horses while Clint continued to have a look around.

"Anything?" Tom yelled.

"No," Clint called back, without looking up, "doesn't look like anybody walked here."

Clint walked back to Tom and the horses.

"I thought you said people swam here?"

"They do."

"I don't see any indication of that," Clint said. "Somebody was here, but it wasn't to swim. They rode in, did something—talked, maybe—and rode out."

"To where?"

"Looks like three riders, and when they left they went in different directions."

"Could have nothing to do with Ted."

"You're right," Clint said. "I'm going to pick one trail and follow it, see where it leads me."

"Could go nowhere," Tom said.

"You don't have to come."

"No, no," Tom said, "my old man told me to stay with you. Let's go."

They mounted up, picked one trail and started off after it.

\*\*\*

"I thought you were a tracker?" Tom asked.

"I can track," Clint said, "but I'm no expert. This trail just disappeared."

"Well, the ground *is* pretty hard here," Tom said, giving Clint an excuse.

"Yeah," Clint said, looking down at it with disgust.

The trail had led them away from the swimming hole, and had not gone toward town, or the Horton place. Like

Tom had said, it could have had nothing to do with his brother. On the other hand, 3 riders could have met there to discuss kidnapping Ted.

"You want to ride back to the swimming hole?" Tom asked.

"No," Clint said, "let's go to town."

"What do you want to do there?"

"Well," Clint said, "for one thing I want to talk to the sheriff."

"My brother Tim?" Tom asked. "Why? He's useless."

"He's the sheriff," Clint said. "Let's see what he knows."

"He don't know much," Tom said. "He sure don't know how to pick a wife."

"It's just something I want to check off my list," Clint said. "After all, he's the law."

"Yeah, well, we're not gonna get much from him," Tom said, "but let's go."

\*\*\*

When they reached town, Tom led Clint directly to the Arrowhead Saloon. They dismounted, and Tom tied off his horse.

"Ain't you gonna tie yours?" he asked.

Clint dropped Eclipse's reins to the ground.

"He's not going anywhere."

"Somebody might take it into their head to steal him," Tom warned.

"I'd like to see them try," Clint said. "Like I said, he's not going to go anywhere, on his own or with anyone else. He's going to stay right here and wait for me."

"That's some horse."

"Yeah, he is."

They mounted the boardwalk and went through the batwing doors. The interior was as empty as it had been the day before, the first time Clint walked in. There was just Benji behind the bar, and a man at a back table with his head down.

"Just like I figured," Tom said, and they walked toward the table.

# Chapter Fourteen

"Beers, gents?" Benji called.

"Yeah, bring them over," Clint replied.

They reached the table and Tom shook the man by the shoulder.

"Tim!" he said.

The man didn't move.

"Come on, Tim." He shook him again.

Benji came over with the beers, set them down next to the full whiskey bottle.

"How long's he been drunk?" Clint asked.

"All his life, I guess," Benji said, "but he ain't drunk now."

"What?" Tom asked.

"Yeah, see? The bottle's still full. He hasn't had a drink, yet."

Benji walked away.

"Tim!" Tom yelled. "Hey, Tim?"

"Sheriff!" Clint chimed in.

Suddenly, the man sat up, his eyes wide, and looked around him.

"What the hell—" he said.

Clint and Tom sat opposite him.

"That's what I say," Tom replied. "What the hell are you doin'?"

"Well," Tim said, "I *was* sleepin'."

"You're supposed to be tryin' to find our brother," Tom said.

"You are the law, aren't you?" Clint asked.

Tim squinted at Clint.

"Who's this?"

"Meet Clint Adams."

Tim looked surprised. Now that he was awake Clint could see the family resemblance. He wasn't as thin as his father, and not as beefy as his brother.

"The Gunsmith?"

"That's right," Tom said.

"What the hell are you doin' here?" Tim asked.

"Are you asking me that as the sheriff?" Clint asked.

"Sheriff!" Tim spat. "That job ain't gonna last long, now that we have a police department."

"The job wouldn't last long anyway, not the way you're doin' it," Tom said.

"Well, it ain't all of us who have Pa's trust to run the business, is it?" Tim asked.

"I don't run the business," Tom said.

"But you will."

"I'm not here about who runs the business, Sheriff," Clint said.

"Why the hell *are* you here, then?"

"Your father asked me to help find your brother, Ted."

"Then why ain't you out with the rest of the town?"

"Because I'm working on a different idea."

"What idea is that?"

Tim pushed his untouched beer toward his brother.

"Try that and stay sober for ten minutes," he said.

Tim grimaced, but drank some of the beer down.

"I'm assuming Ted didn't wander off in a daze," Clint said. "I'm thinking he went off by himself because he wanted to, or he was grabbed."

"Grabbed? By who?"

"I don't know," Clint said. "I was going to ask you to suggest somebody."

"Like who? An enemy of my father?"

"Could be."

"Take your pick," Tim said. "Everybody in town hates the old man."

"Present company included?" Clint asked.

Tim finished the beer, slammed the mug down and said, "Oh yeah."

# Chapter Fifteen

"I don't hate him," Tom said to his brother.

"Yeah, you do."

The two brothers glared at each other.

"Well," Clint said, "how about somebody who isn't family?"

"Like I said," Tim replied, "the whole town."

"Give me somebody specific," Clint said. "Maybe a business rival?"

"He's got lots of those," Tom said.

"Locally?"

"Not all of his businesses are local," Tom said.

Clint drank some beer. Benji brought over another one for Tom, who gave him the full bottle of whiskey.

"Hey!" Tim objected.

"Take it away," Tom said.

The bartender took it back to the bar with him.

"So neither of you can suggest anybody?" Clint said. "Somebody who'd want your father to be dealing with this instead of doing business."

"Ask daddy's favorite, here," Tim said. "I don't know nothin' about the business."

"Oh, shut up!" Tom said. He looked at Clint. "Let me think about it."

"Yeah, okay."

Clint stood up.

"Where are you goin'?" Tom asked.

"To talk to the other law in town."

"That fucking chief of police?" Tim asked.

"That's him," Clint said, and left the two brothers, still glaring at each other.

\*\*\*

He entered the station and told the policeman sitting there, "I'd like to see Chief Collins."

"Does he know you, sir?"

"Yes, he does," Clint said. "Tell him Clint Adams wants to see him."

"Clint . . . Adams?" the young officer said. "The, uh, Gunsmith?"

"That's right."

"I heard you was in town."

"Can you tell him?"

"Oh, sure," the man said. "just wait here."

The officer went to the back of the building and returned quickly.

"He's in his office," he said. "He, uh, said you know the way."

"I do. Thanks."

Clint made his way to the chief's office and knocked on the open door.

"Come in," Collins said, from his desk. "Have a seat. So you're still in town."

"I am," Clint said, sitting.

The chief sat back in his chair.

"What's on your mind?"

"I agreed to help Cyrus Horton find his son, if I can," Clint said.

"Good," Collins said. "We can use all the help we can get."

"I have some questions."

"Ask."

"How much do you know about Cyrus Horton's business dealings?" Clint asked.

"Not much. Why?"

"You've got people out there looking for a man who wandered off in some kind of daze," Clint said. "I'm taking a different approach."

"That he left on his own, with his head working perfectly?" Collins asked.

"No," Clint said, "that he was taken."

"What would lead you to think that?"

Clint shrugged.

"Why should I just go the same way as everyone else?" he asked. "Cyrus is a rich man. Somebody grabs his son and can demand anything."

"There hasn't been a ransom demand, yet."

"Ted's only missing since yesterday, right?"

"That's right."

"There's still time," Clint said.

"So you're thinking they're going to ask for money?" Collins asked.

"Or something else."

"Like what?"

"Something to do with Cyrus' businesses," Clint said.

"Oh, so you think this was done by a business rival."

"It's a possibility."

"Do you have anything else?"

"I took a ride to a swimming hole that Ted liked," Clint said.

"And?"

"Found some tracks."

"People go there to swim."

"This looked like three men rode there, dismounted, talked, and then rode away."

"So they met there to plan a kidnapping?"

"Like I said," Clint replied, "a possibility."

"What would you like me to do?" the chief asked.

"Well, if you don't know anything about his business, just do what you're doing," Clint said. "And maybe one of us will get lucky."

"I hope so."

Clint stood up but didn't leave.

"I spoke with the sheriff."

"Tim Horton? Really? He was awake?"

"Yes," Clint said, "and sober."

"What did he have to say?"

"That everybody hates his father," Clint said, "including him."

"Then maybe he had something to do with it."

"Now there's another possibility," Clint admitted. "He also accused his brother Tom of hating their father."

"You've met the whole family."

"Almost," Clint said. "Haven't spoken to or even seen Tim's wife, yet. But pretty much all the others."

"Tim's wife," Collins said. "Wendy."

"That's right."

Clint thought he saw something flicker in the man's eyes.

"Why not?"

Clint shrugged.

"She just wasn't around," he said, "but I'll get to her."

"Well," Collins said, "let me know if you find out anything, or if I can help."

"I'll do that, Chief," Clint said. "Thanks."

He went back to the front of the building, waved to the young officer, and left.

# Chapter Sixteen

Clint headed to his hotel.

He was glad Cyrus Horton had not offered him a room in his house. There were too damn many people there as it was.

He had almost reached his hotel when he realized how hungry he was. So he kept walking until he came to a small restaurant called the Main Street Café, the kind of place he preferred to eat.

After a meal he felt better and started for his hotel. Then he got an idea and changed direction once again. He went to Hank Skinner's little shop, found it open for business.

"You're not wearin' a shirt you bought from me," Skinner said from behind his counter.

"Sorry," Clint said. "I'll get to it tomorrow."

"I'm just funnin' with you," Skinner said. "What's goin' on with you?"

"Seems I'm going to be staying in town longer than I thought," Clint said.

"Why's that?"

"Mainly because of my inability to mind my own business," Clint replied.

He told the man about his meeting with Cyrus Horton, and his agreement to help the man find his son.

"Sounds to me like you got a hankerin' to help people," Skinner said. "What's wrong with that?"

"Ah, it usually gets me into trouble."

"What can I do to help?"

"You seem to know a lot about what goes on in Carthage," Clint observed.

"I keep my ear to the ground, and my eyes open," Skinner said. He waved at the interior of his empty store. "I don't have much else to do."

"Tell me about Cyrus Horton."

"Rich man, family man, was devastated by the death of his wife—so devastated that he brought home a new one soon after. A young one. His kids aren't happy about it."

Clint wanted to say, "Neither is his wife," but kept silent.

"As for his business, he's a deadly, cut throat businessman who has made a lot of enemies."

"In town?"

Skinner nodded.

"He's put some people out of business. But I'm sure there are those in other places, as well. His domain stretches far and wide."

"Someone told me his family hates him."

Skinner smiled.

"Nobody in town would tell you that, so you probably talked with his son, Tim—our sheriff."

"You're right."

Skinner nodded.

"He feels he has reason to hate his father," the older man said.

"Does he?"

Skinner shrugged.

"Only he knows that, for sure."

"And the rest of the family?"

"Who knows?" Skinner said. "They're so busy fightin' with each other over the old man's affection and attention, when would they have time to hate him?"

"I don't know," Clint said, shaking his head. "I've been running into some odd families lately, and this seems to be another one."

"Are families odd?" Skinner asked. "I don't know because I don't have one."

"Neither do I," Clint said, "but believe me, with the things I've seen, I don't think we're missing anything."

# Chapter Seventeen

This time Clint did go back to his hotel. He found Tom Horton waiting in the lobby.

"Where's the sheriff?" Clint asked.

"Where do you think?" Tom asked. "His head hit the table before I was out the door. Where've you been?"

Clint told Tom about his talk with the Chief. He left his visit to Skinner out. He was keeping the older shop-keeper as his hole card, in this game.

"I thought you'd be gone by now," Clint said.

"Pa said for me to stick with you."

"That's why I thought you'd be gone."

"There's a smaller saloon right down the street. How about another beer?"

"Sure, why not?"

They walked only half a block to a place called simply, THE SALOON.

The inside was as empty as the Arrowhead had been, without the added charm of the sleeping sheriff. They each got a beer from the bar and carried it to a back table.

"Do you have any family?" Tom asked.

"No."

"No brothers, no wife?"

"None."

"But you had a father."

"Yes, but he's been dead a long time."

"Did you love him? Did he love you?"

"I suppose so."

"Which way?"

"Both."

"Well, I love my father, Adams," Tom said. "But that doesn't mean I don't hate him, sometimes."

"You seemed to resent that when your brother implied it," Clint said, "and the name's Clint, by the way."

"Tim didn't imply it, Clint," Tom said, "he came right out and said it."

"Yes, he did."

"Well, he's got no right," Tom said. "He should only be worried about his own relationship with Pa."

"What about the rest of the family?" Clint asked. "When did everyone start hating everyone?"

Rather than saying Clint was wrong, and everyone *didn't* hate everyone, Tom took a sip of his beer and then said, "Probably when Ma died."

"Or was it when he brought Elizabeth home?"

"Well, that surprised the hell out of us all," Tom said. "When he went to St. Louis we thought he was still in mourning, and the trip would do him good. We didn't think he'd come home married."

"He was already married to her when they got home?"

"Oh yeah," Tom said, "they did it in St. Louis."

"So does everyone in the house dislike her because Cyrus married her or because of her personality?"

"Probably both," Tom said. "Look, there's somethin' else you need to know."

"What's that?"

"Tim and I take after Pa," Tom said, "but Ted, he takes after our mother."

"How, exactly?"

"Well . . . girls liked him. He's . . . pretty." Saying that word seemed to pain Tom.

"I thought you said they didn't like it when he watched them swim?" Clint said.

"They didn't," Tom said. "They would've liked it if he stripped down and swam with them."

"I see," Clint said. "Of course, you mean except Eloise?"

"I hope so," Tom said. "Our family is goin' through a hard time, but we don't need to add . . . what's it called?"

"Incest?"

"Right."

Tom went back to his beer.

Clint knew that Eloise liked sex. But . . .

# Chapter Eighteen

They ordered fresh beers.

"I said I needed time to think about your question," Tom said.

"About your father's business rivals?"

"Yeah," Tom said. "He didn't have any."

"You mean—"

"I mean nobody could match him," Tom said, cutting Clint off. "When he wanted to put somebody out of business, he did; when he wanted to buy somebody's business, he did; when he wanted to beat somebody, he did."

"He never failed?"

"Never."

"Tell me," Clint said, "how involved is Hardesty?"

"Will manages things when Pa's away."

"But you think you can," Clint said, "Or should."

"I know I can," Tom said. "I don't know that I should."

That surprised Clint.

"Don't get me wrong," Tom went on, "I think the job should be mine, but Will's had it for a while. I don't expect my Pa to just fire him and hand the job to me."

"That's very understanding of you," Clint said. "How do you get along with Hardesty?"

"Fine, I suppose," Tom said. "But I don't like that he's got his hat set for Eloise."

"You told me Hardesty liked Ted," Clint said. "What about the other way around."

"Ted liked everybody," Tom said. "That was a problem."

"How do you mean?"

"He'd take home a stray dog that bit him," Tom said. "And he'd let the damned thing bite him again."

"I see."

Clint frowned. That sort of personality supported the prospect that somebody took him, or lured him, away. But it also supported the fact that he might not have been right in the head. He was hearing different things from different people, and it was almost as if he was looking for more than one man.

"So he doesn't have a girlfriend?" Clint asked.

"No."

"Not one girl that he particularly liked?"

"Well . . . there is a girl in town he talks about," Tom said, "but she's young."

"How young?"

"Sixteen."

"And he's twenty-two?"

"Yes."

"Not so young," Clint said. "What's her name?"

"Shirley . . . something."

"You don't know?"

"No," Tom said, "he was just always talkin' about Shirley."

"Always? Sounds like he might be serious about her."

"How could he be?" Tom asked. "Ted can't be serious about anythin'."

"I'd like to talk to the girl, anyway."

"Well, I don't know where to find her and I don't know her last name," Tom said.

"Do you know what she looks like?"

"I may have seen her once," Tom said, "but I don't remember . . . I think she had blonde hair."

"A sixteen year old blonde," Clint said. "Shouldn't be too hard to find."

"Maybe he mentioned her to Eloise," Tom said. "I can ask."

"Good," Clint said, "you do that." He didn't want to see Eloise again—not yet, anyway.

"Now?"

"Yes," Clint said. "I'll stay around town and ask some questions."

"Of who?" Tom asked.

Clint shrugged.

"I'll think of somebody."

# Chapter Nineteen

They left the saloon and split up.

"I'll see you later tonight at the Arrowhead," Tom said. "Maybe Tim will be awake."

"I'll be there," Clint said.

As Tom started to cross the street, a group of men came riding in. They stopped to speak briefly with Tom, and Clint could see the man in the lead was Will Hardesty. The exchange did not look friendly, and then Tom stalked away.

As the riders started forward again, Clint stepped into the street, blocking their path.

Hardesty stared hard for a moment, then recognized him.

"Adams. You're still here?"

"Mr. Hardesty," Clint said. "I thought by now you'd know I was working to help your boss."

"Well, yeah," Hardesty said, "yeah, I do." He turned to his men. "You fellas can get a drink and fresh mounts. We'll be goin' out in an hour."

They grumbled but nodded.

"One drink!" Hardesty reminded them, as they rode on.

"How about a beer?" Hardesty asked Clint.

"I think I'd rather have some coffee," Clint said, having just had a few beers with Tom.

"I know where we can get either," Hardesty said, "or both."

He rode his horse over to the hitching post, tied it off, and then started walking. Clint fell into step.

"The boss says you're takin' a different direction than the rest of us," Hardesty said.

"Yes," Clint said. "I'm assuming he didn't just wander off."

"Who have you talked to about Ted?"

"Everyone, I think," Clint said. "Oh, except for Tom's wife, Cassie."

"You'll get an attitude from her, and probably not much more," Hardesty said.

"An attitude?"

"Yeah, she's a bitter woman. If you talk to her she'll just complain about Tim, and everybody else. You talk to Eloise?"

"I did."

"She's somethin', isn't she?"

"She is that."

"But she has an odd opinion of her brother Ted," Hardesty said. "So you have to take what she says lightly. Here we go."

Hardesty took Clint into yet a third saloon in town. It was tiny, just a long rectangle, no tables just a bar, which at the moment was empty.

"Still plenty of people out searchin'," Hardesty said. "Sam, a beer and a coffee."

The pleasant looking bartender said, "Comin' up, Will."

"Plenty of people out looking," Clint said, "but apparently no bartenders."

"Bartenders have to stay behind the bar," Hardesty said. "They don't belong anyplace else."

The bartender came, put a glass mug in front of Hardesty, and a mug of coffee in front of Clint. He looked about 30, Hardesty's age.

"Find 'im yet?" he asked.

"Not yet."

The man shook his head. Then walked to the other end of the bar.

"So if you talked to a lot people, you're gettin' a lot of different pictures, ain'tcha?"

"Two or three," Clint admitted.

"Well, let me give you the real picture—"

"—as you see it, you mean."

"No, no," Hardesty said, "I'm gonna tell you about the real Teddy Horton."

"So far," Clint said, "I haven't run into anyone who's called him Teddy."

"You see?" Hardesty said. "Already I'm showin' you how people lie. Almost everybody calls him Teddy."

"His father?"

"No."

"Brothers?"

"Well . . . sometimes."

"His sister?"

"All the time."

Not in Clint's presence.

"And the boss's new wife," Hardesty said. "She called him that and she made it sound . . . dirty."

"And Cyrus doesn't notice?"

"You can't tell him anything bad about Elizabeth," Hardesty said. "He only sees the good in her, and as far as I can see, that takes some real hard lookin'."

"You think she married him for his money?"

"What else?" Hardesty asked. "Why would a beautiful young woman marry an older man but for money?"

"For love?" Clint asked.

Hardesty laughed.

"This woman only loves herself," he said, "believe me."

"Do you think she might have something to do with Ted missing?"

"No," Hardesty said, right away.

"That's pretty definite."

"She'd have no reason," he said. "She gets whatever she wants just by askin'."

"What about the others?" Clint asked. "His brothers? His sister? Any of them have a motive?"

"No," Hardesty said, "not them. Look, I said I was gonna give you the truth about Teddy."

"Right, right," Clint said. "Go ahead. Paint me a picture of the real man."

Clint sipped his coffee, prepared to hear about another Ted Horton—this one called Teddy.

# Chapter Twenty

Back at the house Tom dismounted and left his horse in front. He went inside, dodged the people there, and went upstairs to his sister's room and knocked.

"Lisa, it's Tom."

"Just a minute."

He heard movement inside, and then finally the door opened. She looked disheveled.

"What were you doin'?" he asked.

"Sleeping," she said. "What do you want?"

"To talk."

"About Teddy?"

"Yes."

"I don't know where he is," she insisted.

"I know that. Just let me come in."

"Fine."

She backed away and allowed him to enter. She said she had been in bed, but the bed was made.

"What do you want, Tommy?"

"I'm workin' with Clint Adams," he said.

"Why?"

"Because Pa told me to."

"Naturally," she said. "Good little boy, always does what Pa says."

"We're looking for Ted, Lisa."

"Yeah," she said. "Whataya want from me?"

"Ted used to talk about a young girl in town," Tom said. "I think she has blonde hair, is about sixteen. I think her name's Shirley—"

"Not Shirley," Eloise said, cutting him off, "it's Sally. Her last name's Bennett. She's seventeen and she's always been nice to him. You think he left with her?"

"I don't know," Tom said. "Clint just asked me about him and girls."

"Well, Sally's the only one Teddy ever talks about," Eloise said, "even though others have flirted with him. Including our dear step-mom."

"What?"

"Come on," she said, "don't tell me you didn't know. She flirts with all three of you. Why do you think Cassie and Wendy hate her so much?"

"That's crazy."

"You're just too stupid to know what she's doing," Eloise said.

"Hey!"

"Don't take it personal," she said. "It's just because you're a man."

"I don't have time for this now," Tom said. "I have to go back to town and tell Clint about Sally."

"Fine, go," she said. "See what Sally knows."

"And you?" he asked, at the door. "Are you gonna stay in your room the whole time he's gone?"

"Maybe!" she snapped. "Shut the door!"

# Chapter Twenty-One

Clint spent a couple of hours walking around town, stopping people and asking questions. Some would talk to him, some wouldn't. But they all seemed to have heard he was in town and knew who he was.

However, whether they spoke to him or not, he didn't get anything helpful. Finally, he headed for the Arrowhead Saloon to meet once more with Tom Horton.

***

When Clint arrived, Horton was standing at the bar. It had grown dark, and many of the searchers had returned and were taking up space at the bar, or at tables. He checked in the back, though, and saw Sheriff Tim sitting with his head down on the table, as usual.

"Tom," he said, joining him at the bar.

"Beer!" Tom called to Benji, who returned with two icy mugs.

"Did you talk to Eloise?" Clint asked.

"I did," Tom said. "I had the girl's name wrong. It's Sally. Her last name's Bennett. She's seventeen. About all I had right was the color of her hair."

"Did Eloise tell you where to find her?"

Tom didn't bother telling Clint that he hadn't asked that question.

"No."

"That's okay," Clint said. "We'll find her." Clint studied Tom. "You look bothered. What happened with Eloise?"

"Ah, as usual she got my goat," Tom said. "She's good at that."

"All women are good at that," Clint said. "What did she have to say?"

"She claims Elizabeth has been flirting with the three of us since she and my Pa came back," Tom said. "Can you believe that? Why would she do that in front of my Pa?"

"Maybe she doesn't do it right in front of him," Clint said.

"She don't do it, at all!" Tom insisted.

"Did she get your goat because she said you don't notice it?"

Tom frowned and grumbled.

"She said I don't notice 'cause I'm a man!" Tom finally replied. "What the hell does that mean?"

"Men are stupid when it comes to women," Clint said.

"You really believe that?"

"I do," Clint said, "but I also believe that women are stupid about men."

"Well," Tom said, "if you're gonna put it that way, it sounds fair."

Clint waved Benji over.

"Another beer?" the barkeep asked.

"A question," Clint said. "You know a family in town called Bennett?"

"I know a fella named Bennett," Benji said, "comes in here every once in a while. Clyde Bennett. Has a few whiskeys, doesn't seem too anxious to go home. I don't think he's got a very happy life there."

"Does he have a daughter named Sally?" Tom asked.

"Sure does, pretty little thing," Benji said. "I think that's part of his problem. She drives him kinda crazy."

"Do you know where he lives?"

"Naw," Benji said, "I know lots of men who come in here night after night, but I got no idea where they live. Sorry."

"That's okay," Clint said, "thanks."

"I just thought of somethin', though," Benji said

"What's that?"

"I seen him drinkin' once in a while with Jimmy Gates."

"Why do I know that name?" Tom asked.

"Jimmy gets in trouble from time to time," Benji said. "But he's outta jail right now."

"Is he in here tonight?"

"Not yet," Benji said, "but he will be."

"In that case," Clint said, "two more beers."

# Chapter Twenty-Two

"There he is," Benji said, coming over to Clint and Tom. "Just walked in."

They both turned and look at Jimmy Gates, who was greeted loudly by a group of men at the other end of the bar.

"Who are they?" Clint asked.

"His friends," Benji said. "More troublemakers."

"Why would this fella Bennett drink with him?" Clint asked. "Is he a troublemaker?"

"He'd like to be," Benji said, "but he's got a wife and daughter that keep a tight rein on him."

"I get it," Clint said.

"You ever been married?" Tom asked.

"No."

"Then you don't get it."

Clint shrugged.

"Benji, give that man a beer, on me," Clint said, "tell him I'd like to talk with him."

"Right."

Benji drew the beer and carried it down to Jimmy Gates. They exchanged words, and then Gates accepted the beer, said something to his friends, and walked over to Clint and Tom.

"You Adams?" he asked.

"That's right."

"Thanks for the beer," Gates said. He was in his late 20s with the kind of unearned swagger young men of that age developed. Clint wondered why he would drink with someone like Clyde Bennett, who, judging by the fact that he had a 17 year old daughter, was considerably older than Gates.

"Don't mention it."

"What's it for?" Gates asked, sipping it.

"Answering a few questions."

"This got to do with that missing Ted Horton?"

"It does."

"Don't know why I should help the Hortons," Gates said. "but a beer's a beer, so go ahead. Ask your questions."

"You know a fella named Clyde Bennett?"

"Yeah, I know Clyde," Gates said. "Tries to drink with me and my friends sometimes. I guess he thinks it'll make him feel younger and not married. See, Clyde, he's kinda henpecked."

"So I heard," Clint said. "I need to talk to him. Do you know where he lives?"

"Yeah, I know." Gates didn't offer though. Just sipped his beer.

"Mind sharing that information?" Clint asked.

"For a beer?"

"What else do you want?" Clint asked.

"Don't pay him nothin', Clint," Tom said. "We'll find this Bennett ourselves."

Gates looked at Tom.

"I tell you what, Horton," he said. "I'll give ya the information for free. You just remember this to your Pa, huh?"

"Yeah," Tom said, "I'll remember."

"Bennett lives on Kimball Street," Gates told Clint. "House with two broken shutters on the front windows."

"No address?" Clint asked, hoping that shutters hadn't been fixed of late.

"We ain't that good a friends," Gates said, "although I wouldn't mind goin' over there and visitin' his tasty little daughter."

"Do you know Sally?" Clint asked.

"Naw, naw," Gates said, "she's too good for me and my friends. Real stuck up, ya know? She's lucky we don't much care. There's plenty of other fillies in town."

"Well," Clint said, "I'm much obliged for the information, Mr. Gates. Benji, make sure Mr. Gates gets another beer on me."

"Sure thing," Benji said.

"Thanks, Adams," Gates said. "You're okay for a washed-up legend."

Gates laughed and went back to his friends.

"You gonna let him talk to you that way?" Tom asked.

"We got other things, to worry about, Tom," Clint said. "Come on."

\*\*\*

As Gates reached his friends the 4 men slapped him on the back because they'd heard his closing remark.

"You were right, Jimmy," Del Reed said. "Adams is washed up."

"That don't mean beatin' him to the draw wouldn't still make somebody famous," Gates said.

"You really think you could beat him?" Reed asked.

"I could beat him," Denny Munson said.

"You can't even beat me, Denny," Gates said.

"Can too."

"Then let's have it out tomorrow," Gates said. "Winner gets to go after the Gunsmith."

"What, you and me shoot it out?" Denny asked. "Jeez, Jimmy, you're my friend."

"Not to the death, you idiot," Gates said. "We'll shoot at some targets. Prove who's better."

"That sounds good," Paul Kendall said, "but do it later in the day, will ya? I gotta work tomorrow."

"Tomorrow afternoon," Gates said to Munson, "that empty lot on Sackett Street."

# Chapter Twenty-Three

Clint and Tom made their way over to Kimball Street. It was a neighborhood of small houses away from the lighted main streets. They had to cross some railroad tracks to get there, which would put Bennett and his family squarely on the wrong side of the tracks, as the saying went.

"The better houses in town have two floors and electric lights," Tom said. "I ain't ever been to this neighborhood. How do people live like this?"

"Not everybody was born with a silver spoon in their mouth like you, Tom," Clint said. "They take what they can get."

"Seems to me if they worked hard enough for it," Tom responded, "they'd get more."

"Well," Clint said, "I have to say this Clyde Bennett sounds like a man who'd rather drink and complain than work harder."

"Then he deserves what he gets," Tom said.

They started looking for a house with two broken shutters.

"Jesus," Tom complained, "all these houses have broken shutters."

"Yeah, but we're looking for two shutters in the front. Like there." He pointed.

"How the hell did Ted ever meet this girl?" Tom wondered.

"Did he ever come to town on his own?"

"Well, yeah, he wasn't no prisoner or nothin'."

"Did he ever go to a dance or church social?"

"Probably."

"There you go," Clint said. "He could have seen her at a dance in a pretty dress."

"Or at that swimmin' hole," Tom said, "wearin' nothin'."

"That, too."

They went through the broken gate, up a walk of chipped stone tiles to the front door and knocked. The door was answered not by Clyde Bennett, but by a faded looking woman in her 40s who stared at them pleasantly through the screen door.

"Can I help you fellas?" she asked in a friendly tone. This didn't seem like the kind of woman a husband would be drinking to run away from.

"Mrs. Bennett?" Clint asked.

"That's right."

"My name is Clint Adams and this is Tom Horton."

"Horton?" She stared through the screen. "Well, land sakes, what's a Horton doin' on this side of the tracks?"

"We're lookin' for my brother Ted, Ma'am."

"That poor boy that's missin'?" she asked.

"Yes," Tom said.

"Do you know him, Mrs. Bennett?"

"I don't think I've ever had the pleasure," she said. "But why wouldja be askin' me that?"

"We heard that Ted knows your daughter, Sally," Clint said.

"Oh, I don't think so," she said, shaking her head. "Where would Sally meet one of the Hortons?"

"At a dance, maybe?" Clint asked. "Is she home? Would we be able to talk to her?"

"Well . . ."

"We were also looking for your husband," Clint added.

"Oh, him," she said, and the friendly look left her face. "He's out drinkin' somewhere so he don't have to come home."

"What about Sally?" Clint asked. "May we talk with her?"

"Well . . . I suppose so," she said. "Come on in."

They opened the screen door and entered the house. It was small and cramped, but very clean. Clint noticed that the woman's dress was simple and looked homemade.

"I'll get her," Mrs. Bennett said. "She's in her room."

"Thank you."

Tom looked around the house.

"I couldn't live like this."

"Don't start that again," Clint said. "Just be polite to the lady."

"Yeah, yeah."

When she came back she was leading a young girl in another handmade dress. But where her mother was faded, this girl had a glow to her. She was blonde, but her hair was the color of straw rather than the gold of Eloise's hair. She was slender and extremely pretty.

"Sally, these gentlemen wanna ask you some questions," her mother said. "This is Mr. Adams, and that's Mr. Horton."

"Hello."

"Hello, Sally," Clint said. "Thanks for talking to us."

"Mama said I should."

"Can I get you fellas some coffee?" Mrs. Bennett asked.

"Yes," Clint said, "that'd be real nice."

"Have a seat," she said. "You ask Sally your questions while I get it."

Clint and Tom sat on the threadbare sofa in the center of the room, while Sally sat on a matching chair across from them. She primly placed her hands in her lap.

"Sally," Clint said, "we're looking for Ted Horton. Tom is his brother."

She stared at them and didn't say a word. She just stared at them.

# Chapter Twenty-Four

Looking at her, Clint wondered if this girl was as simple as he had been told Ted Horton was?

"Do you know Ted Horton, Sally?"

This time some expression came over her face, but it was only one of mild interest.

"I've seen him in town," Sally said, "but I don't know him."

"Has he ever . . . bothered you?" Clint asked.

"Not really," she said, as her mother came in and handed each man a cup of coffee. "I think he was watchin' me at the swimmin' hole once, but he didn't do anythin'."

"You never told me that!" her mother said. She looked at Tom. "Does your brother do that often? Watch girls at the swimmin' hole?"

"He did," Tom said. "We've stopped him from doin' it anymore. He never meant no harm, he just wanted to look."

"But . . . that's positively indecent!"

"Yes," Clint said, "it is. That's why the family took steps to stop it. But . . ." he looked at Sally, ". . . he's been missing since yesterday."

Now she looked interested.

"I heard some talk in town about search parties, but I didn't know . . . I'm sorry to hear that."

"So, you haven't seen Ted since yesterday?"

"Mr. Adams," she said, "I haven't seen Ted Horton in . . . well, I can't remember that last time I saw him. In fact, I don't think I've seen a man in a blue shirt for days."

Mrs. Bennett's coffee was weak, but Clint took a sip before setting the cup down and standing up.

"Then we'll be on our way," he said. "I'm sorry if we bothered you ladies."

Sally stood up and her mother hurried to stand by her side.

"Your brother isn't gonna come after my Sally, is he?" she asked Tom. "That ain't why you came here, is it?"

"No, Ma'am," Tom said. "Don't worry, Ma'am. He's not comin' here."

"Good-night," Clint said to both of them, and left the house with Tom.

"What do you think?" Clint asked, when they were outside.

"About what?"

"Her lying."

"What makes you think she was lying?" he asked.

"She was way too calm," Clint said. "And what color shirt was Ted wearing when he went missing?"

"I don't know. Why?"

"She said she hasn't seen a man in a blue shirt in days," Clint said. "If Ted was wearing a blue shirt, how would she know unless she had seen him?"

"So we need to find out what color shirt my brother was wearin'."

"You were out looking for him," Clint said. "Nobody said what he was wearing?"

"Not to me, but I know my brother when I see him," Tom pointed out.

"You're right," Clint said, "but your father would've given the chief of police a description. Let's go ask him."

"Where?"

"The police station."

"Will he be there this late?"

"I hope so," Clint said.

***

"The Chief ain't here."

Clint looked at the young police officer, who appeared to have been sleeping when they walked in.

"What's your name?"

"I'm Officer Jenkins."

"Where is he?" Clint asked.

"Well, he could be out lookin' for the missing man, or he could be home."

"Tell me something," Clint said, "do you know who the missing man is?"

"Yeah," the young man said, "Ted Horton."

"This is Tom Horton, Ted's brother," Clint said.

"Well," the man said, "all our men are out lookin' for him."

"But you're here, Jenkins," Clint said. "Why?"

"The Chief wanted somebody to be here all night, just in case," Jenkins said.

"Okay," Clint said, "will you tell us where the Chief lives?"

"If I did that," Jenkins said, "I'd get fired."

"Do you know who this is?" Tom asked, pointing at Clint. "This is Clint Adams, the Gunsmith."

"I, uh, know that," Jenkins said, nervously. "You ain't gonna shoot me, are ya?"

"No," Clint said. "I'm not."

"You can see the Chief in the mornin'," Jenkins said. "I'll tell 'im you were here."

"Okay." Clint looked at Tom. "Let's go."

As they turned to leave, Clint stopped and turned back.

"Jenkins, do you have a description of Ted Horton?"

"Sure do," Jenkins said, "right here on the desk.   But . . . don't you know what he looks like?"

"We do," Clint said, "but what color shirt is he wearing?"

Jenkins picked up the piece of paper looked at it, then said to Clint, "Blue."

# Chapter Twenty-Five

"So what now?" Tom asked, as they left the police station. "Do we go back and call her a liar?"

"No," Clint said, "we keep an eye on her, see where she goes."

"You think she'll go to him?"

"Maybe," Clint said. "Maybe she's got him stashed somewhere, maybe he's hiding and she'll bring him food."

"But . . . what's he hidin' from?" Tom asked.

"I don't know," Clint said. "His family? Something he did?"

"What could he've done?"

"Could be something nobody knows about, yet," Clint said.

"Like what?"

"What would he think was so bad he'd have to hide out?" Clint asked.

They were walking back toward the lighted part of town.

"Maybe he stole somethin'?" Tom suggested.

"Has he ever stolen anything before?"

"Not that I know of," Tom said.

"That might be our problem," Clint said. "There's something going on we don't know about."

"So how do we find out?"

"By following the girl."

"I guess I could do it," Tom said.

"No offense, Tom," Clint said, "but you're too big. You'd be noticed. And I have to keep poking around to find out what this is all about."

"Then who?"

"You tell me," Clint said. "This is your town. Is there anybody here who can follow somebody without being seen?"

"I don't know . . ."

They reached the lights and sounds of the main street and Clint stopped walking. The saloons now seemed to be in full swing, but he was suddenly very tired.

"Well, think it over and have an answer for me tomorrow morning," Clint said.

"What if she goes to see him tonight?" Tom asked.

"I don't think she will," Clint said. "Not after we were just there questioning her. At least, let's hope not."

"All right," Tom said. "Where do you wanna meet tomorrow mornin'?"

"My hotel," Clint said.

"Breakfast?"

"I'll bet you can get a better meal at home than any-where in town," Clint said.

"Yeah," Tom said, "but I'd have to eat it with the whole family."

"Okay then," Clint said, "breakfast."

\*\*\*

When Tom Horton got back to his father's house—for his father always let it be known it was *his* house—he found it oddly empty and silent. By morning, however, searchers would be back seeking orders from Cyrus Horton as to where to look next.

It was dark, but not late, so he was surprised not to see someone walking around—his father, sister, maybe even Tim. Although his brother was the town sheriff, he spent little time at the jailhouse, and when he did sleep in a bed—and not in the Arrowhead Saloon—it was home.

Tom stood just inside the front door, listening, but didn't hear any movement. Then the voice came.

"Tom."

His father was standing at the front of the hall that led to his office. The slender older man moved very quietly.

"Pa."

"Come to my office and tell me what's been goin' on," Cyrus said.

"Yes, Pa," he said, and followed.

\*\*\*

Clint sat in his room and wondered where Clyde Bennett was? The word he'd gotten on the man was that he sometimes tried to drink with Jimmy Gates and his friends, but that wasn't the case tonight. Yet Mrs. Bennett—he'd never gotten her first name—was sure he was out drinking.

Sally Bennett's demeanor, and mention of a blue shirt, made him fairly sure she was involved in Ted's disappearance somehow. However, that still didn't clarify if he was willingly missing, or not.

If he had left under his own power, then maybe it was to run away with Sally. How would her father and mother have reacted to that? Could something have happened between Ted and Clyde?

A fight?

Or worse?

Had one of them killed the other?

Could that have been why Ted was in hiding?

Or was that why Clyde Bennett wasn't home?

He decided he had 2 things to do in the morning. Get somebody to follow Sally Bennett wherever she went and find Clyde Bennett.

Those decisions made, he decided to turn in.

# Chapter Twenty-Six

When Clint came down the next morning Tom Horton was waiting in the lobby, looking decidedly unhappy.

"What happened to you last night?" he asked.

"I'll tell you when we're at a table with very strong coffee," Tom said.

"Suits me."

They went into the hotel diningroom and told the waiter the ham-and-eggs had to be good, and the coffee had to be strong.

"Yes, sir."

Tom's eyes were red-rimmed, as if he had been up all night. They didn't talk until the pot of coffee was on the table and they each had a cup. Neither of them diluted it with sugar or cream.

"All right, Tom," Clint said, "what's going on?"

"My father, that's what," Tom said. "He was waitin' for me last night when I got home."

"I think I know what was on his mind."

"Yeah, you'd think you would," Tom said. "Do you know what he said to me?"

"What?"

"To stop wastin' time and find my brother."

"What makes him think we've been wasting our time?" Clint asked.

"My father thinks anythin' that's not makin' him money is a waste of time."

"Did you tell him what we've been up to?"

"Yes."

"And?"

"He told me to forget it," Tom said, as the waiter set their plates down.

Clint found himself ravenous and dug in immediately.

"Why?"

"He says Ted either wandered away in a daze, or has been kidnapped," Tom said. "He refuses to accept that he may have gone on his own, or that he's involved with some girl."

"From the other side of the tracks?"

"Any girl," Tom said, "from any side of the tracks."

"I see."

"He wouldn't listen to reason," Tom said. "He refuses to believe Ted might have left on his own. He thinks his sons know they're all better off here."

"Aren't they?"

"For now, but I have my own plans. I don't know about Tim. And Ted . . ." He shook his head.

"We'll have to ask him when we find him," Clint said. "Now tell me who you thought of to tail Sally?"

***

After breakfast they had another pot of coffee.

"Are you sure about this man?" Clint asked.

"No, I'm not sure," Tom said. "But he's a slippery character who can stand in front of a mirror and not leave a reflection. That should be good enough."

"Where did you get that mirror comment?"

"You'll never guess," Tom said. "Sheriff Tim."

"How did he get involved?"

"He was having breakfast at the house with Pa, Elizabeth and Eloise. I pulled him aside and asked him."

"So this person has been recommended by Tim?"

"Yeah."

"And you trust his judgment?"

"When Tim was first given the sheriff's job he was pretty good at it."

"Then what happened?"

"Then the town fathers—including my father—decided we needed a modern police department."

"Ah," Clint said, "so that's what changed him?"

"As soon as Chief Collins got appointed, Tim just . . . gave up."

"All right," Clint said, "so what's this fella's name?"

Tom put his cup down and said, "Henry Skinner."

"Skinner?"

"That's right."

"But Skinner's an old gent who has a small clothing store in town," Clint said. "Are you sure your brother wasn't pulling your leg?"

"He says Skinner was a slippery character before he hurt his leg. Now he has a store, and Tim says nobody ever notices him."

Clint could understand that. Skinner looked like an older, harmless gentleman who people wouldn't give a second look to.

"Okay, then," Clint said, "I'll go and talk to him. As it turns out, he and I met soon after I came to town."

"Pa still wants me to stay with you," Tom said. "What do you want me to do?"

"You can come along, but I'll go in and talk to him myself. We get along, Skinner and me."

"Fine by me," Tom said, "but I don't need any new clothes."

Tom dressed like he was going to be on the trail. Clint wondered if, when he was doing his father's business, his clothes were better, more expensive?

"Let's go, then," Clint said. "The quicker we get somebody on Sally, the better."

# Chapter Twenty-Seven

Skinner looked up from his counter when Clint entered, and smiled.

"Back for more shirts?"

"No," Clint said, "I'm back to ask for your help."

"Really? With what?"

"I need somebody followed."

"And you thought of me?"

"No, you were recommended to me," Clint said.

"By who?"

"The sheriff."

"Tim Horton? Really? I thought he wasn't doing much as a sheriff, these days."

"He's not," Clint said, "but he mentioned you to his brother Tom, who mentioned you to me."

"And why me?" Skinner asked.

"Well, according to Sheriff Horton," Clint said, "you were once a pretty slippery character, until you hurt your leg."

Skinner acquired a rather sheepish look.

"Slippery?"

"Yes," Clint said. "According to him, you could stand in front of a mirror and not have a reflection."

"I suppose I should take that as a compliment," Skinner said.

"Does that mean that at one time you were on the wrong side of the law?"

"Let's say I once made my livin' by my wits and leave it at that."

"What about my favor?"

"Follow someone?" Skinner asked. "Who?"

"A young girl named Sally Bennett."

"I know Sally and her family."

"Well then," Clint said, "maybe you can't help me. If they know you—"

"No, no," Skinner said, "I said I know them, they don't know me. What are you hopin' to—oh, wait, are you thinkin' she's gonna lead you to Ted Horton?"

"Hopefully," Clint said.

"Do you think she kidnapped him or lured him away?"

"I don't know," Clint said. "Maybe they're young lovers planning to run. Who knows? Can you do it? I mean, with your leg?"

"There are certain things I once did that I can't do anymore because of my leg," Skinner said, "but this should be easy."

"Can you get on it today?" Clint asked. "Hopefully she's still in her house."

"I'll get right over there."

Clint was surprised at how spryly Skinner came from behind his counter.

"You're moving pretty well for an old guy," he observed.

Skinner smiled.

"My leg's not as bad as it looks," he said, "and I'm not as old as I look."

\*\*\*

Clint told Skinner where he could find him—either at his hotel or the Arrowhead Saloon—and then left.

"So?" Tom asked.

"He'll do it."

"Good. Now what?"

"Now," Clint said, "we have to find Clyde Bennett."

"Where do we start?"

"Let's talk to Mrs. Bennett again," Clint said, "see if he came home."

\*\*\*

"No, she said, at the door, "he never came home."

"Can you tell us where he works?"

"Who says he works?" she asked. "You'll probably find him in a saloon or a whorehouse."

"Can we talk to Sally for a moment?"

"She's busy with chores."

"Mrs. Bennett, are you worried that your husband didn't come home?" Clint asked.

"No," she said, her pleasant demeanor completely gone, "it might even be better for us if he never did."

She closed the door in their faces.

***

As they walked away Clint saw Tom looking around.

"What are you looking for?" he asked.

"Your guy," Tom said, "Skinner. Ain't he supposed to be here waitin' for Sally to come out?"

"If he's any good," Clint said, "he's here and we can't see him."

"So then, what next?"

"Let's do what the lady suggested."

"And that is?"

"Check saloons and whorehouses," Clint said. "Do you know where they all are?"

"Oh, yes."

# Chapter Twenty-Eight

They checked 3 saloons—leaving the Arrowhead for later—before Clint had Tom take him to a whorehouse.

"Which one?" Tom asked.

"How many are there?" Clint asked.

"Half a dozen," Tom said. "Carthage is still growin'."

"How different are they?"

"Real different," Tom said, "you got the real expensive ones, and then you got the nickel-a-poke ones."

"How many are nickel-a-poke?"

"Two."

"Considering where Bennett lives," Clint suggested, "let's try those first."

"For that," Tom said, "we gotta go across the tracks, again."

"I don't have a problem with that," Clint told him. "Seems to me Bennett would be more comfortable there."

"I don't know," Tom said, "his house was small and rundown, but the inside was clean."

"Let's find out if that makes a difference to him," Clint said.

\*\*\*

Tom took Clint to the first nickel-a-poke house across the tracks, but several streets away from Bennett's house. It was close enough, though, that the man could sneak out to it whenever he wanted.

"Looks worse than it is," Tom assured Clint, as they stood in front of a dilapidated 2 story house.

"You've been inside?"

"I had to get Tim out of there once," Tom said, "you know, before the sheriff got caught sampling the merchandise."

"Oh, I see. Guess the town and his wife wouldn't have liked that."

"Not much."

Clint let it go at that. They went up the walk and knocked on the front door. It was opened by a blowsy looking redhead in a filmy nightgown. She stood leaning on the door with her hip and head cocked. She had a body that used to be firm and nice but had gone to seed so that now she looked a bit doughy. But Clint was sure she knew how to do her job.

"Help you, boys?" she drawled.

"Yes," Clint said, "we're looking for a man named Clyde Bennett. We were wondering if he was here with one of your girls?"

"Well, honey, if you wanna find that out, you're gonna have to come in and look for yourself. See, don't matter how long a fella's lived here in town, when he comes here he don't use his real name."

Tom looked around to see if anyone on the street was watching them.

"You comin' in?" she asked.

Clint looked at Tom, who said, "yeah, sure, why not?"

She backed up and they entered. Then she turned and faced them in the hall. To the right was a sitting room with several girls lounging on sofas and chairs with men. The furniture all had cushions that were showing stuffing.

"Well," she asked, "do you see him?"

"We don't really know what he looks like," Clint said, "but we have an idea." The men in the sitting room all seemed to be too young to have a 17 year old daughter. "None of them looks like him."

"What about upstairs," Tom said. He took a step toward the stairway behind the girl, but she blocked his path.

"Sorry, you can't go up there without a girl, and you can't have a girl unless you pay."

"But we don't want girls," Tom said. "We just wanna find the man we're lookin' for."

"Alicia," a woman's voice called out, "what's goin' on?"

An older woman wearing a green dress approached them. She had a lot of black hair that fell down around her bare shoulders. If this was the madam of the hen house, Clint was surprised at how beautiful she was. She appeared to be in her 40s but did not have the doughy look to her skin that Alicia did.

"Why are you keeping these gents out here in the hall?" she asked.

"Oh, Mrs. Chill, they're just lookin' for a friend of theirs. They wanna know if he's here. But I told them they can't go upstairs without a girl."

"Alicia, these gents are not interested in going upstairs with a nickel-a-poke girl. You can go. I'll take care of them."

"Yes, Ma'am."

"Gents, follow me, please. We can talk in my office."

"Thank you," Clint said.

She led them down a hall and into her office closing the door behind them. The room was furnished expensively, which was not expected, given the way the rest of the place looked.

"Well, gentlemen," she said, "my name is Caroline Chill and I run this establishment. And you are?"

"Clint Adams."

"Tom Horton."

"Mr. Horton," she said, raising her expertly trimmed eyebrows, "you're on the wrong side of the tracks, aren't you?"

"Yeah, a bit," Tom admitted.

"And you, Mr. Adams," she said. "Isn't the Gunsmith also on the wrong side?"

"Seems to me you're on the wrong side of town, Mrs. Chill," Clint said. "This place seems way beneath you."

"Thank you for the compliment," Chill said, "but I happen to be right where I belong. Tell me what I can do to help you? Are you the law—oh wait." She looked at Tom. "You're looking for your missing brother, aren't you?"

"We are, but that ain't why we're here," Tom said.

"Then why are you here?" she asked.

"We're looking for a man named Clyde Bennett. He actually lives a few streets from here."

"Ah, Clyde," she said. "Yes, he comes in."

"Alicia told us that men don't use their real names here in Carthage," Clint said.

"That's true, but I tend to know the locals," she said.

"Is he here, then?" Clint asked.

"Not at the moment."

"Was he here last night?"

She nodded.

"Most of the night. Trudy said he talked her ear off and gave her two nickels."

"No poke?" Clint asked.

"No poke."

"Do you know where he spends his days?" Clint asked.

"Not at home, that's all we know," Chill said.

"We?"

"That's what he told Trudy," she said. "He didn't want to go home. Sad, really. A man should always want to go home."

"Would Trudy know where he is?"

"No," Chill said, "last night was the first time she'd ever been with him. He doesn't have a regular girl here, so he doesn't tell them much."

"Would he be at any of the other whorehouses?" Clint asked her.

"Maybe," she said, "but if I was you I'd try Miss Buffets." She pronounced it boo-fay.

"Why her place?"

"It's the other nickel-a-poke house in town. Bennett wouldn't be able to afford any of the other places."

"All right," Clint said, "thanks for the advice."

"I'll show you out."

At the door Clint thought of another question.

"Tell me something else, Miss Chill," he said. "Was Bennett here two nights ago?"

"No," she said, "not at all . . . and next time you come by, just call me Caroline."

# Chapter Twenty-Nine

"Wow," Clint said, when they were out on the street. "She is operating way below herself."

"You think so?"

"I know so," Clint said. "That's a lady, Tom."

"Really?" Tom asked. "She sort of reminds me of Elizabeth, my Pa's wife."

"That so? Then I guess Elizabeth is a lady, too."

"Not that I noticed," Tom grumbled. "Whataya wanna do now?"

"Get something to eat," Clint said, "then go to this other whorehouse run by—what was it—Miss Buffet."

"Melody Buffet," Tom said.

"You know her?"

"We went to school together."

"How did she end up running a whorehouse?"

"Her family was poor," Tom said. "She didn't have much choice when it came to jobs."

"So she worked her way up," Clint said. "Or down, whichever way you look at it."

They started walking.

"Why do you wanna eat?" Tom asked. "Didn't we just have breakfast?"

"That was hours ago, Tom," Clint said.

"Hours?"

Clint nodded.

"At least two."

\*\*\*

But all Clint needed was a cup of coffee and a piece of pie. It was Tom who ordered a bowl of beef stew in the small café they stopped in.

"Hey, this ain't bad," Tom said, because—technically—they were still on the wrong side of the tracks.

"This pie's pretty good, too," Clint said. "Tom, it still seems to me that something's on your mind. Did your father say anything else?"

Tom let his spoon drop into the bowl and stared across the table at Clint.

"Yeah," he answered, "he said he thought Ted must be dead, if he ain't been found by now."

"What?"

"And he's gonna have some of the men go to the swimmin' hole and . . . check for his body."

"They're going to dive down and look for it?"

"Yeah," Tom said, "but it ain't all that deep."

"So, would finding him dead be preferred by your father to finding out that he just . . . ran off?"

"You don't know the old man, Clint," Tom said. "He can't stand the idea that any of the family would leave. He won't *let* us leave. That's why Tim and me, we still live in the house, even though we're married."

"Wouldn't it be odd if it was Ted who was the first to break away?"

"That's the one the old man won't ever get over," Tom said. "He thinks Ted is his fair-haired, innocent boy—not as ambitious as I am, not as dumb as Tim is."

"And Eloise?"

"Not as hardheaded."

"Ah . . ."

Tom picked up his spoon again.

"To tell you the truth, I was glad when he told me to stick close to you," he said. "Otherwise he would've had me out there with the rest of the town beating the bushes."

"And while all this goes on he stays home, in his office?" Clint asked.

"Yeah, he says from there he's, uh, co-ordinatin' the search."

"Why bring me in, then?"

"Because you're here," Tom said. "You're the best at what you do, and my father likes to hire the best."

"But what I'm best at doesn't come into play here."

"On the chance that Ted was kidnapped," Tom said, "it does."

"Well," Clint said, "I'm not planning on shooting anyone."

"You don't ever plan on it, do you?"

"No," Clint said. "And I don't do it unless I have to."

"And when do you usually have to?"

"When somebody's trying to kill me."

# Chapter Thirty

When they finished eating, Tom took Clint to the building that housed Miss Buffet's Cathouse. Like the other nickel-a-poke house, it looked ready to fall down.

This time Clint agreed to let Tom do the talking, since he knew Melody Buffet. When they knocked, the door was answered by a small brunette in a threadbare nightgown.

"We'd like to see Miss Buffet," Tom said.

"If you want girls you'll have to—"

"Not girls," Tom said, "Miss Buffet."

"But—"

"Tell her it's Tom Horton."

"Wait here." The girl closed the door in their faces.

"You've never been here before?" Clint asked.

"No," Tom said. "I've seen Melody a time or two in town, though."

When the door opened again it was the same girl.

"Come with me."

As they followed her through the house Clint noticed she was barefoot and had some scabs on her feet.

"In here," she said, stopping at an open door.

"Thanks," Tom said.

Tom and Clint entered the room and a brunette woman Tom's age stood up from behind a desk. She was wearing an off-the-shoulder pink gown.

"Tom," she said, coming around, "how nice."

She gave him a big hug and then looked at Clint.

"And who's your handsome friend?"

"Melody, this is Clint Adams. He's helpin' us look for my brother, Ted."

"Yes, I heard Ted was missing," she said. "That's too bad, but how can I help?"

"We're looking for Clyde Bennett," Tom said. "We heard he might be here."

"He is," she said. "He spent the night, which he does every so often."

"I didn't know you rented your girls out by the night."

"No girl," Melody said, "just a bed. We do that sometimes for regular customers—especially the ones who don't want to go home."

"Can we see him?" Tom asked.

"I don't care," Melody said. "He should be awake and out of here by now. If he's not I'm gonna charge him extra. You can tell him that. He's upstairs in room 4."

"Thanks, Melody."

"I hope he can help you find Ted," Melody said. "I haven't seen much of him in recent years, but I remember he was a cute little kid."

Tom nodded, turned and started out the door with Clint.

"And you fellas," she called after them, "don't mind all the naked girls up there."

\*\*\*

They went up the stairs, dodged the naked girls in the hall who all but ignored them because they weren't working yet. A couple of them smiled at Clint, though. Naked they didn't look bad, Clint thought, but he wondered if their clothes would be less than stellar?

"Room 4," Tom said, pointing.

"Let's not knock," Clint said, and opened the door.

Bennett was on his back on the bed, with a girl crouched between his legs, sucking his cock. When Clint and Tom entered both he and the girl got to their knees.

"Don't tell Miss Buffet," the girl said, "please, I was only, uh, trying to wake him up."

"Well," Clint said, "looks like you succeeded."

She grabbed her robe, held it over her thin frame, and ran past them out into the hall.

"That cost me a nickel!" Bennett complained. "I didn't get to finish."

"You can take that up with Miss Buffet, Bennett," Clint said. "Right now you have to deal with us."

"Whataya talkin' about?" he demanded. "Who're you?"

"I'm Tom Horton, this is Clint Adams."

"Oh," Bennett said to Clint, "I heard you was in town." Then he looked at Tom. "And I heard you was lookin' for your brother, but what's that got to do with me."

"Bennett," Clint said, "we think your daughter has taken up with Ted Horton, maybe is even hiding him."

"What? Naw! Taken up with—whataya mean? Do you mean—" Bennett started to ask, appalled.

"That's what we mean," Clint said. "Did you know anything about it?"

"I don't know nothin'!" he squawked. "But my wife, she knows everythin' Sally does. You oughtta talk to her."

"We did, Clyde," Tom told him. "We already talked to your Mrs. and Sally."

"Oh Lord," Bennett said, covering his face, "what'd my Mrs. Say?"

"She's not real happy with you," Clint said. "She said she didn't care if you never came home."

"Aw, hell, she don't mean that," Bennett said. "She's a sweet ol' gal sometimes."

"Why don't you go home then?" Tom asked.

"Well," Bennett said, "'cause she's a sweet old gal *some* of the time!"

# Chapter Thirty-One

They left Bennett in the room getting his trousers on.

"He comin' down?" she asked, at the bottom of the stairs, "Or do I hafta get my bouncer to go up and get 'im?"

"He's comin' down, Melody," Tom told her. "It was good to see you."

"You come back when you're wantin' a poke, why don't you?" she said. Then she looked at Clint. "'specially your handsome friend here."

"We'll keep that in mind, Miss Buffet," Clint said.

"Aw, honey, you can just call me Melody."

"Thank you, Melody. You have a good rest of the day."

"The rest of the day's gonna be filled with fellas who can only afford a nickel-a-poke," she told him. "That ain't the makin's of a good day."

Clint tipped his hat, and he and Tom left the house.

"She was a pretty little thing when we was kids," Tom said. "Kinda faded now."

"Aren't we all?" Clint said.

\*\*\*

"What now?" Tom asked, as they returned to a more populated part of town.

"I doubt that man could have or would have done anything to your brother, especially not because of Sally. He doesn't seem like a doting father."

"So I guess we'll have to wait and see if we hear anythin' from Skinner."

"I don't want to just sit around and wait," Clint said. "Maybe your father's heard something."

"A ransom demand?"

Clint nodded.

"Would he pay it?"

"In a minute."

"And where's Hardesty?" Clint asked.

"He's at the swimmin' hole," Tom said.

"I tell you what," Clint said, "I'll check the swimmin' hole, and you go check with your father."

"Sure you don't wanna do that the other way around?"

"I'm sure," Clint said.

Just in case they did find Ted's body in the swimming hole, Clint thought it was better if he was there instead of Tom.

They headed for the livery stable.

\*\*\*

Clint rode up to the swimming hole, which had half a dozen men around it, and a couple in the water. He spotted Hardesty and rode over to him.

"Anything?" he asked, dismounting.

"Not yet. What've you got?"

Clint told Hardesty about Sally Bennett and about talking to Clyde, her father.

"Any chance she was meeting with Ted in secret and her father killed him for it?" Hardesty asked. "Maybe dumped him here?"

"No chance," Clint said. "Not that there's no chance his body is here, there's just no chance he was killed by Clyde Bennett."

Hardesty stared out at the water.

"He's not here," he said.

"How do you know?"

"We've gone through it already, twice," the manager said. "But I had that feelin' even before we came out here."

"So where do you think he is?"

"Gone," Hardesty said. "I think he saw a chance and lit out, got away from his father and the family."

"Why?"

"Because they all treat him like he's an idiot," Hardesty said.

"And he's not?"

"I don't think so," Hardesty said. "He may not be as smart as Tom, but he's not a dummy."

"Why leave without his horse?"

"I don't know," Hardesty said. "I guess we'll have to ask when we find him."

# Chapter Thirty-Two

Clint decided to stop at his hotel before meeting Tom Horton at the Arrowhead Saloon.

"Where have you been?"

Clint turned, saw a woman sitting on a chair just inside the door.

"I've been a little busy," he said. "Do I know you?"

She stood up, looked to be in her late 20s and when the word "angular" came to him to describe her, he figured out who she was.

"You're Wendy, Tim's wife."

"That's right," she said. "Shall we go up?"

"Up?"

"To your room," she said. "We have some business."

"Do we?"

"I'll tell you when we get there."

She headed for the stairs, and he followed her. When they got to his door she stepped aside and tapped her foot impatiently while he unlocked the door. She was tall, with beautiful auburn hair, and smelled sweet. In profile her chin looked pointed, but he could see she had more curves underneath the pretty black dress she was wearing than she showed when you looked at her head on.

He closed the door and turned to face her. She smiled, which made her pretty all of a sudden.

"Well, Mrs. Horton—"

"Wendy," she said, "call me Wendy."

"All right, Wendy," he said, "what business do we have?"

She turned and strolled about the room with her hands behind her back.

"I had a talk with Lisa."

"Lisa?"

"Eloise," Wendy said. "She prefers to be called Lisa."

"You and she, you get along?"

"As much as anyone in that family does, yes," she said. "After all, you do need some sort of an ally in life, don't you?"

"Yes, I suppose you do."

She turned to face him.

"She told me what you and she did."

"What we . . . did?"

"Yes," she said. "You know, all the sex."

"Well . . ."

"That's what I want to talk to you about."

"Sex?"

"Why, yes," she said. "What did you think I wanted to talk about?"

"Well," he said, "I thought maybe you knew something about Ted."

"Ted? That moron?" she said. "He's wandered off. They'll find him, eventually. No, I'm not worried about Ted."

"Tim, then?'

"Sheriff Tim?" she asked. "My husband is more useless as a man than he is as a sheriff. No, no, I need a man. That's why I've come to you."

"Wendy—"

She moved closer to him.

"I don't mean to shock you, Mr. Adams," she said, placing her hands on his chest, "but I want sex."

"I don't think—"

"I'm very good," she said. "I know I'm not as pretty as Eloise, or Elizabeth, but I know what I'm doing in bed."

"I'm sure you do—"

"No, you're not," she said, sliding her hand down the front of his pants, "but you will be, after."

She rubbed her hand over him, and the situation—and her scent—was making him react.

"Mmm, there," she said, "I've . . . aroused your interest."

"What if your husband finds out?"

"Don't worry," she said, unbuttoning his trousers, "he won't mind. Do you know what he told me one night when he couldn't satisfy me?"

"Hmm? What?"

"That maybe I should go and work in one of the whorehouses if I wanted sex," she told him. "Maybe even one of the cheap, nickel-a-poke ones. Oh, not because that's all I'm worth, I assure you, but because I'd get more sex that way." She reached into his underwear and took hold of his hardening cock. "Ooh, I can see Eloise wasn't exaggerating."

"Wendy—"

"Do you want to take off your gun?" Wendy asked. "Here, let me help you."

She unbuckled his gunbelt, then turned and hung it on the bedpost.

"Eloise told me you like to keep it close. Now, where were we? Oh, yes . . ."

She pulled his trousers and underwear down to his ankles, so that his cock flailed about.

"Oh, your boots," she said. "Why don't you sit down and take them off while I take off my clothes?"

She pushed him down to a seated position on the bed and then started to undo her dress. He worked his boots off while watching her, and when she was naked she stood directly in front of him and posed with her hands on her hips.

"Not all that bad, huh?"

She was obviously one of those women who looked better naked than dressed. Her skin was lovely and pale, her breasts small but firm, with dark, insistent nipples pointing at him.

"Not bad, at all," he agreed.

She laughed and threw herself on him.

# Chapter Thirty-Three

They rolled about on the bed, naked, and got better acquainted. They had more time for that than he and Eloise had, because there was no danger of anyone walking in on them.

She still had some sharp angles in bed—hip bones, elbows and knees—but made up for it with her breasts and nipples, her butt, and the soft, wet mound between her legs. And, yes, her skills.

He kissed her, and their mouths melded together. There was nothing awkward about it, even though it was their first kiss. It went on longer and she employed her tongue as well. Kissing her was one of the most pleasant things he had ever done.

Her body was hot, supple, and seemed to fit up against his perfectly. He enjoyed the feel of her hard breasts and nipples against his chest.

She ran her hands over his body, caressing, probing, all with care and knowing. Whatever Wendy had done before meeting Tim, marrying him and coming to Carthage must have been interesting, to have given her this kind of bedroom prowess. Idly, as he ran his lips over her shoulders, neck and breasts, he wondered if she had ever been a whore?

J.R. Roberts

But when his lips found her hard nipples and she gasped, she reached down and grabbed his hard cock and all thoughts fled from his mind.

Now it was only feeling, and tasting, and smelling . . .

\*\*\*

Later, she further displayed her talents by sliding down between his legs and taking him into her hot mouth. This had been done to Clint many times before, but Wendy was doing it with very special care and attention to the head, the shaft, and the sack. At times she was working on two, or all three, at the same time and it was all Clint could do not to explode into her mouth. But even more than that, he wanted this session to continue—for her sake, and for his own enjoyment.

She continued to suck him and, at one point, seemed to detect that he was holding back. She gave all of her attention to working him with her mouth, sliding her hands beneath his buttocks and holding him tightly, digging her nails in.

Finally, the movement of her head, the feel of her lips and tongue, her insistent hands, all combined to practically yank the explosion out of him . . .

\*\*\*

"Your husband's a fool," he said to her later. She was lying next to him with her head on his shoulder.

"I know," she said. "I've told him that. And now you understand that it's not always about looks, eh?"

"There's nothing wrong with your looks, Wendy," he told her.

"Oh please," she said. "I live in a house with three beautiful women. And you've seen all that Eloise has."

"She could learn a few things from you," he said.

"That's what I've told her," Wendy said. "Eventually, I think I'll get through to her."

"And Cassie?"

She laughed.

"Oh, I'll never get through to her," she said. "The only thing she and I have in common is our dislike for Elizabeth. But that won't last, either."

"Is she going to change?" Clint asked.

"She's going to leave."

"How do you know?"

"Just watching her, you can see the itch to get out," she said.

He didn't bother telling her that Elizabeth had admitted as much to him.

***

Later, before she left, she got onto her back and spread her legs for him.

"Hard," she said. "I'm afraid it's going to have to last me a while."

"I'll do my best to make it memorable," he promised.

And he did—his best, that is. Whether or not it was memorable was going to be up to her.

He got between her spread legs, leaned over her and slid right into her wet pussy. When he started to fuck her, hard and fast, she smiled, said, "Oh yes!" and wrapped her legs around his waist.

He kissed her mouth then, while he was fucking her, then her breasts and nipples.

"Bite harder!" she said. "Even if you draw blood, who's going to know but me?"

He didn't want to draw blood, but he did as she asked and bit harder, sucked harder, fucked hard as she urged him on and on.

He lasted for as long as he could before finally releasing himself inside of her and hoping that he had been able to give her what she wanted, something she could remember for a long time.

As he would.

# Chapter Thirty-Four

"No ransom," Tom said, when he met Clint at the Arrowhead. "What about you?"

"Nobody at the swimmin' hole," Clint said. If that fact put Tom's mind at ease, he didn't show it.

"You look done in," Tom said. Clint had just walked in and joined him at the bar. "Have a beer."

Clint didn't want to tell Tom that he was done in from trying to satisfy his brother Tim's wife's sexual urges.

"I'll take it," Clint said.

Benji put the beer in front of him and he drank half of it down, gratefully.

There were a few other customers in the place, including Sheriff Tim at his usual table, in his usual position.

"Doesn't your brother ever get tired of just sitting?" Clint asked.

"No," Tom said, "but you know, I sort of understand poor Clyde Bennett when I think about my brother."

"How's that?"

"Tim doesn't want to be home with his wife. She's always naggin' him to be a man."

"I'd think that would make him want to act more like a man, or a sheriff."

"She wants him to be more of a man in the bedroom, if you know what I mean."

"I think I do."

"You know," he said, lowering his voice, "she once tried to get me into bed."

"No!" Clint had to act surprised.

"Not that she ain't good-looking, sort of, but I got a wife of my own to satisfy. Wendy's Tim's job."

"A job he apparently isn't doing very well."

"Which pretty much makes three jobs he's not doin' well," Tom observed.

"Three?"

"Husband, sheriff, and son."

"What about brother?"

"Well," Tom said, "we're all fallin' down on that job."

"So if and when Ted comes home, do you plan on being a better brother?"

"Oh, no," Tom said, "I've got enough trouble tryin' to be a good son and husband."

"And what about Eloise?"

"Same difference," he said. "She's not a real good daughter or sister, but at least she doesn't have to try to be a good wife."

Clint knew something else Tom's sister was good at.

At that point 3 men came through the batwing doors, laughing and backslapping, obviously having already be drinking elsewhere.

"Where is he?" one of them said aloud.

"There, at the back table," another said.

"That's the sheriff?" the third man asked.

"That's him," the first said.

"Looks like trouble," Clint said, to Tom. "Should we wake your brother? Warn him?"

"Just watch," Tom said.

The 3 men walked across the saloon floor, watched by the few customers who were drinking, who didn't seem very concerned.

"Do you know them?" Clint asked.

"I've seen them in town," Tom said. "And I think they applied for a job with us, but Hardesty turned them away."

"Looks like they might want to take it out on the sheriff," Clint said.

"That's part of his job, ain't it?" Tom asked. "Handling drunks like that?"

"If he's awake," Clint said.

"Like I said," Tom replied. "Just watch."

***

"Hey there, Sheriff!"

Tim didn't move.

The 3 men looked at each other.

"Is he dead or sleepin'?" one of them asked.

"Shit, Hal, I dunno," the first said.

They looked at the sheriff again.

"Hey, Sheriff!" the first man shouted. This time he reached out, put his hand on the man's shoulder and shook him. "Sheriff!"

Suddenly, Tim's head sprang up off the table. His hand reached out, grabbed the man by the front of the shirt and pulled. The man's head slammed into the table and he slumped to the floor, unconscious.

Tim sat back and stared up at the other two men.

"You fellas want somethin'?" he asked.

They could see the sheriff's badge shining on his shirt.

"Uh, no, Sheriff," Hal said, "we don't want nothin'."

"Then pick your friend up and get the hell out of here," Tim said.

"Yes, sir," the other man said. "We'll do that."

Both men picked up the unconscious man and dragged him to the door. As they went out, another man came walking in. Clint saw that it was Chief Collins, but the man was not wearing a uniform.

When Clint looked back at Sheriff Tim, he once again had his head down on the table.

# Chapter Thirty-Five

"I don't understand," Clint said.

"I don't think Tim does, either."

Collins came walking over to where Clint was standing.

"Mr. Adams, Mr. Horton," he said, "what went on in here?"

"Just my brother doin' his job, Chief," Tom said. "He ran those three drunks out of here before they could cause trouble."

"Is that a fact?" Collins asked, frowning.

"It is," Tom said. He picked his beer up from the bar. "I'll leave you two to talk."

He walked to an empty table not far from his brother's and sat.

"Is that what happened?" Collins asked.

"It is," Clint said, "and he handled the situation without ever pulling his gun."

"Interesting," Collins said. "Sounds like the kind of man I need for my department."

"You never know," Clint said. "Beer?"

"Please."

Clint signaled Benji for two more.

"I heard you were looking for me," Collins said.

"I was, but they wouldn't tell me where you live."

"Well," Collins said, "my man was only doing his job." He picked up the beer and sipped it. "Is there something I can do for you?"

"I had a question," Clint said, "but I managed to find the answer."

"But you haven't managed to find the missing man?" the Chief asked.

"Not a sign. You?"

"Not yet," Collins said. "I understand his father is having the swimming hole searched."

"Two or three times already," Clint said. "No sign of a body."

"Well, that's good news," Collins said. "Of course we're all hoping to find the boy alive."

"Yes, we are," Clint said.

Collins looked over at Tom.

"How are you and the older son getting along?"

"Pretty good," Clint said. "He seems to want to find his brother for their father's sake."

"Don't we all," Collins said. He took another sip of the beer, then set it down, obviously done with it. "I better get going. My wife will be wondering where I am."

"Oh, you're married?"

"Didn't I mention that?"

"No, you didn't."

"Well," Collins said, "it's not germane to the work, is it?"

"I guess not."

"Good-night."

"'night, Chief."

As the chief went out the batwings, Benji came over and looked at the beer mug, which had only two sips missing from it.

"Somethin' wrong with my beer?" he asked.

"I just think beer isn't the chief's drink."

"No wonder I ain't never seen him in here before," Benji said, taking the mug.

Clint picked up his own beer and walked over to Tom's table.

"I don't like that man," Tom said. "You?"

"The jury is still out." Clint sat. "I'm still interested in what your brother just did. I thought everybody was saying how useless he was."

"Oh, he can be useful when he wants to be."

"And that's not very often?"

"Hardly ever," Tom said.

"So what happened tonight?"

Tom sipped his beer, then said, "They woke him up."

# Chapter Thirty-Six

"If he can do what he did tonight," Clint said, "then why does he turn around and do . . . that?"

Clint jerked his chin in the direction of Tim Horton, who still had his head on the table.

"I mean, I don't even think I've ever seen him have a drink from that bottle he keeps on the table with him."

"He doesn't drink," Tom said. "Hates the taste of whiskey. Will have a beer once in a while, but he ain't a drunk."

"You know," Clint said, "I'm starting to think you like him."

"Listen," Tom said, "I like my brothers and my sister. But we all have to watch our backs with the old man, and that means we don't really have time to watch out for each other. Tim can handle himself and so can Lisa."

"And you?"

"I'm a big guy, Clint," Tom said. "You pointed that out yourself. Yeah, I can handle myself."

"Okay, then, why don't we—" He stopped short when he saw Skinner come through the doors.

"What is it?" Tom asked, turning around.

"We may have something," Clint said.

\*\*\*

Across the street, in an alley, one man held a lighted lamp while a second man—Hal—had a conversation. There was also a third man, but he was on the ground, unconscious.

"What happened in there?" Chief Collins asked.

"He moved fast," Hal said. "Grabbed Jerry's shirt and slammed his head on the table. That was it."

"Did he go for his gun?" Collins asked.

"Never."

"Okay." Collins took out some money and handed it to Hal. "That's for all three of you. Now get out of town."

"But Jerry might need a sawbones," Hal said.

"Hold the lamp closer," Collins told the first man, whose name was Lonny.

Collins bent over Jerry and checked him.

"He's fine, just knocked out. Get him on his horse and out of town. He'll wake up soon."

"Why can't we stay—" Hal started, but Collins cut him off.

"I don't want anybody knowing I hired you to go in there and brace the sheriff. Do you understand?"

"Yeah, we get it," Lonny said.

"And if I see you in town again, I'll throw you in my new jail."

"Okay, okay," Hal said, "we're goin'."

"Use this alley. Don't go back out on the street."

Collins turned and left them there to drag their friend to the rear of the alley, and out of town.

***

Clint told Skinner to sit, went to the bar to get him a beer.

"This is Tom," he said, when he brought it back. "It's his brother we're looking for."

"Hello," Skinner said.

Tom nodded.

"So? You get anything?" Clint asked.

"I went and watched her house, gettin' ready to follow her like you want me to."

"And?"

"Before she could leave the house her father came home."

"He did?" Tom asked. "Didn't seem like he was gonna do that."

"Well, he probably shouldn't't've," Skinner said. He sipped his beer before continuing. "There was a helluva fight between him and his Mrs."

"How do you know?" Tom asked.

"I was across the street and I could hear them yelling at each other."

"What'd they say?" Clint asked.

"I didn't get it all, but she was askin' him why he bothered to come home at all, and he was askin' her something about Sally."

"What about her?" Clint asked.

"Well, I think he was askin' if she was keepin' company with somebody."

"They didn't mention my brother?" Tom asked.

"I didn't hear his name," Skinner said.

"What was the girl doing during all this?" Clint asked.

"Well, I almost missed it," Skinner said, "because I was tryin' to hear what they were sayin', but while they were fightin', she climbed out a back window."

"Did you follow her?"

Skinner looked both annoyed and embarrassed.

"I tried to."

"You lost 'er?" Tom demanded.

"She took off runnin'," Skinner said. "I tried to follow, but with this damn leg I couldn't keep up. So yeah, I lost 'er." He looked at Clint. "I'm really sorry."

"That's okay," Clint said. "You got us something."

"Like what?" Tom asked.

Skinner finished his beer and Clint waved at Tom to be quiet.

"You go on home and get some rest," Clint told Skinner. "I'll talk to you again tomorrow."

Skinner stood up, still looking sheepish.

"There was a time I woulda stayed right with her, you know," he said.

"I know it, Hank. Did she have anything with her?"

"No, she was empty-handed."

"Okay, you go on. And thanks."

"'night," Skinner said to Tom, and left the saloon.

"We shoulda got somebody younger," Tom said. "Somebody who could move."

"Hey," Clint said, "you came up with him, remember?"

"Yeah, but it was my brother, Tim, who told me about him. *Remember*?"

"Yeah, I do."

"So what'd he get us?"

"The girl snuck out," Clint said. "Why would she do that unless she was going to meet somebody."

"And you think it was Ted, and not just some teenage boy?" Tom asked.

"That's what I'm hoping."

"How do we find out?" Tom asked.

"I'm going to watch the house tonight, see if she slips out again. Then I'll follow her."

"What if she left last night, and didn't come back?" Tom asked.

"I doubt that," Clint said. "That's why I asked Skinner if she had anything with her. When she leaves for good I think she'll be taking some supplies with her."

"Do you want me to watch with you?"

"No," Clint said. "Like we've said before, Tom. You're a big guy. We don't want her to spot us. I'll watch and follow her and let you know where we end up."

"Okay," Tom said. "Should I tell Pa anythin'?"

"You can tell him I have a lead," Clint said, "but don't tell him what it is."

"Okay," Tom said, "but that still leaves us with all day tomorrow."

"Maybe some time tomorrow somebody else will stumble onto Ted and this will all be over."

"Do you really believe that?"

"No," Clint said.

# Chapter Thirty-Seven

The next day was wasted.

Who else was there to question? Clint was now working on the assumption that Sally Bennett had something to do with Ted Horton's disappearance, and following her was going to solve that.

Clint had breakfast alone in a town that had once again seemed to empty as volunteers went out. But as the day wore on people began to return earlier than the previous days, as the search began to go stale, with the same ground being covered over and over again.

Clint had lunch with Tom, who gave him an update of the swimming hole search, and his father's mental state.

"Nothing from the swimmin' hole," he said. "Except maybe a lot of mud. They claim they dragged the entire bottom and found nothing."

"I would've thought they'd find something," Clint said. "Even if it was an animal carcass."

"You'd think so," Tom said. "Maybe they're lying to my Pa, except it was Hardesty overseein' the whole thing."

"You don't think Hardesty has ever lied to your father?" Clint asked.

"He probably has," Tom said, "but not over somethin' this big."

"And how's your old man doing?"

"He's growing more and more annoyed."

"At the search coming up empty?"

"At Ted, I think, for causing all this."

"Well," Clint said, "if he was taken, it's not his fault, is it?"

"But my Pa feels that, if he was taken, he would've heard somethin' by now. Why else would anyone take him if not to ransom him back?"

"Good point."

"And he's a little annoyed with you."

"Me? Why?"

"He thought you would have found him by now. He's starting to question whether he should pay you or not. I probably shouldn't have told you that until after you followed the girl tonight."

"Lucky for you and him I'm not doing this for money," Clint replied.

"Why are you doin' it, then?"

He didn't feel like telling another person about his inability to mind his own business because of curiosity, so he said, "Personal reasons."

"Well, don't let the old man get away with not payin' you somethin'," Tom advised. "It's the only way to make him respect you."

"I'll keep that in mind."

"I might as well get out and search," Tom said, "even though I think you might have the right idea about tonight. But I can't just sit around and wait."

"Good luck," Clint said. "Find him and save me the trouble."

"I'll do my best."

\*\*\*

Clint went back to his hotel, thinking maybe he'd just sit in a chair out front and wait. But there were no chairs out front, so he went inside. While he was looking around for a wooden chair, the desk clerk called out to him.

"Uh, Mr. Adams?"

"What is it?" Clint asked.

"Sir, I have a message for you."

"From who?"

"I don't know, sir," the young clerk said. "I found it here on the desk."

The man held out a piece of paper. Clint walked over and plucked it from his hand.

"Thanks. Do you have a wooden chair?"

"Yes, sir."

"Would you put it out front for me, please?"

"Yessir."

Clint waited until the desk clerk went off and came back with a chair, which he set out front. Then he sat on it and looked at the message.

It said: MEET ME AT THE SWIMMING HOLE THIS AFTERNOON AT THREE. I HAVE INFORMATION ABOUT TED HORTON.

It wasn't signed.

He had a few hours to consider the request. It could be a trap, somebody using the missing man situation to ambush him, or it could be somebody with valid information.

He folded the message and put it in his shirt pocket.

# Chapter Thirty-Eight

Clint decided to ride out to the swimming hole and take a chance that the note was legitimate. But he rode out early, circled it, took a good look around, and then got down to the swimming hole first, and waited. Eventually he heard the sound of a horse approaching, then saw the buggy as it came closer to the water.

Then he saw who was driving it.

Elizabeth Horton.

He stood and waited, with Eclipse standing behind him drinking from the water. When the buggy reached him, he played the gentleman and helped her down.

"I'm glad you got my note and came," she said. She was dressed for riding in black pants, a white shirt with a black jacket over it, and black boots.

"Where does your husband think you are?" Clint asked.

"I told him I was taking the buggy out for a ride," she said. "I doubt he actually heard me."

"Well," Clint said, "I'm here because you said you had information for me."

"I do," she said, "but I'm not going to just give it away."

"What?"

"We have to come to an agreement."

"What sort of agreement?"

"I'm a woman married to an old man," she said. "Not just an older man, but an old man. What kind of agreement do you think I'm talking about?"

"Mrs. Horton—"

"Please," she said, taking off her jacket, "you're about to fuck me. Call me Elizabeth."

"Elizabeth—"

She pulled her shirt open, revealing herself to be naked beneath it. Full breasts blossomed, with pink nipples. He was finding it hard to believe that another of the Horton women was baring herself in front of him. Why could these women not find what they wanted—what they needed—at home?

"Elizabeth," he said, looking around, "we're out in the open—"

"Don't worry about that," she said. "My husband's men spent so much time out here with Hardesty that none of them will be coming back."

She leaned back against the buggy and said, "Help me off with my boots before you undress."

Clint decided the safest thing to do was go along with her, so they could get finished and away from here.

He went to her, started to reach for her feet, but she stopped him.

"Now wait," she said, and reached into the buggy. She came out with a blanket. "Spread that for us."

He spread the blanket on the ground and she quickly sat down on it, lifted her feet in the air and wriggled them.

He got down on one knee and helped her off with her boots, all the while aware that her naked breasts were just inches from his head. In fact, he could feel the heat coming from them.

When the second boot came off, he was holding her left foot in his hand, aware of the feel of her skin, and realizing for some reason that her feet were exciting him.

"Now my trousers," she said.

She unbuttoned them, then lifted her butt so he could slide them down over her hips. From there she sat on her bare butt and allowed him to slide them the rest of the way off. Something pink winked at him from behind the dark pubic patch between her legs.

"Now your turn," she said.

She reclined, taking her weight on her elbows, and thoroughly enjoyed watching him undress.

When he joined her on the blanket, naked, he set his gunbelt nearby on the ground.

"You won't be needing that," she told him.

"I'm just playing it safe," he replied.

"If we were playing it safe," she said, reaching out and running her fingertip along the underside of his hard cock, "we wouldn't be here."

\*\*\*

Cyrus Horton came out of his office driven by pangs of hunger to go to the kitchen. Along the way he suddenly wondered where his wife was?

He found the entry hall of the huge house empty, which was odd, given the events of the past few days. Usually there were volunteers there to kowtow to his every whim.

Suddenly, he was aware of Eloise, his daughter, coming down the stairs.

"Father," she greeted. She was dressed for riding, in trail clothes.

"Where are you off to?" he asked.

"Just a ride," she said.

"Are you finally going to look for your brother?"

"I'm not actually going to look for him," she said, "but if I see him I'll certainly give him your best."

"You're an impossible girl, Eloise."

"And I've told you I prefer to be called Lisa."

"Your mother gave you your name," he snapped. "Don't forget that."

"And I never minded her calling me that, but she's gone. I don't want to hear it anymore."

She walked past him, but when she got to the front door he said, "Wait."

She turned.

"Do you know where your step-mother is?"

"You mean your wife, don't you?" she replied. "She's no mother to me, step or otherwise."

"Fine, do you have any idea where my wife is?"

"I was looking out the window a little while ago, saw her drive off in a buggy."

"Oh yes," he said, frowning, "I think she said something about that."

"You ought to pay more attention, Father, when people are talking to you." She opened the door, started out, then turned back. "Maybe you'd start hearing what people are actually saying to you."

"Why don't you just go?" he suggested.

"That's what I'm going to do," she said, "believe me. One day I'm just going to . . . go!"

"That's not very likely!" he shouted after her as she went out the door. "Not as long as you need money!"

# Chapter Thirty-Nine

Why was he finding her feet so exciting?

And it only started there.

He held one foot in his hand, then the other, running his hands over them, and then, abruptly, he kissed the right one, then the left.

"Oh my," she said. "This isn't what I imagined, but . . . oh *my*."

His kisses moved from her foot to her ankle, to her calf, and up her smooth thigh. Just when it seemed he might press his lips someplace wet and warm, he went to the other leg and started again.

Foot, ankle, calf, thigh.

"Oh my," she said, again, and he could feel her smooth skin dapple with gooseflesh.

He ran his hands over her thighs, then spread them and leaned down.

"Oh, yes," she gasped, even before he touched her.

He pressed his face to her pubic patch, then poked into it with his tongue. When the tip of his tongue found her wet slit she jerked, as if struck by lightning.

Elizabeth settled back on the blanket and raised her long legs into the air, spreading them even more for Clint. While he was working her with his tongue and lips, he reached up to pinch her nipples and squeeze her breasts, which were solid in his hands.

After she had trembled and screamed twice—screams that Clint thought could have been heard miles away—he quickly mounted her and thrust his hard cock into her. Now that he had gotten away from her feet—which had oddly mesmerized him—he realized he was going to have to end this quickly. Someone might still come along and find them, especially if they *had* heard her screams.

Because they were lying on a blanket, with only the hard ground beneath them, every time he rammed himself into her he achieved maximum penetration. He didn't really know if she was grunting from pain or pleasure— maybe both. He decided to help her out.

He put his arms around her, rocked back into a seated position, with her sitting in his lap, his cock still inside of her. She immediately started kissing him as they continued to rock together.

They wrapped their arms around each other, kept their lips molded together, and kept her bouncing up and down on his penis, until she was virtually screaming into his mouth. Then and only then did Clint allow himself to ejaculate into her . . .

As they were dressing, Elizabeth said, "Why are you getting dressed so fast?"

"You were pretty loud, Elizabeth. If somebody heard—"

"Don't worry," she said, pulling on her boots, "there's no one around for miles."

He had been watching her put her boots on, but once her feet were covered he turned his attention back to himself and picked up his gunbelt.

Elizabeth slipped into her jacket and then began to try to fix her hair.

"Clint, you can leave," she said. "I need to straighten myself up some more before I go home."

"Haven't you forgotten something?"

She stopped and thought.

"No, I don't think I have."

"You had something to tell me about Ted," Clint reminded her.

"Oh yes," she said, "I did say that, didn't I? Well, I hope you find him."

"That's what you wanted to say?" he asked. "That's why you sent me that message?"

"No," she said, "I sent you that message to get you out here."

"So you lied."

She shrugged and smiled.

"That's what women do, Clint," she said, "to get what they want. And I wanted you."

Clint turned and walked to his horse.

"Oh, don't go away mad, Clint," Elizabeth said. "We could do this again. Or just think of this as me teaching you a lesson about women."

Clint mounted up and turned Eclipse to look at Elizabeth.

"I learned a lesson all right, Elizabeth," Clint said, "but not about women, just about you and how the hatred your husband's children feel for you is deserved."

He turned and rode off, without looking back.

\*\*\*

On a hilltop, just above the swimming hole, Eloise Horton watched as her father's wife fixed her hair, then climbed up into her buggy and started away, presumably heading back home.

But it wasn't going to be her home for much longer.

# Chapter Forty

"Where have you been?" Cyrus Horton asked his wife.

She closed the front door behind her and faced him.

"I told you I was going for a ride," she said.

"Did you?"

"Yes," she said, "but as usual, you weren't listening."

"Don't speak to me in that tone!" he scolded.

Elizabeth looked around. There was no one else present in the hall.

"I'll speak to you any way I like," she said, "when we're alone. It's only when there are other people around that I'll treat you with respect. That was our deal."

"Our deal was for you to offer me comfort," Horton reminded. "I have seen none of that."

"Hey," she said, "I've tried more than once. It's not my fault you're dead between your legs."

"It's not that kind of comfort I'm referring to."

"I'm tired," she said. "I'm going to my room. I'll be down for supper."

He watched as she went up the stairs, and just seconds later the front door opened again and Eloise came in.

"Pa, I'm glad you're here," she said. "I have something interesting to tell you . . .

\*\*\*

Clint was still feeling the exhaustion in his legs from his afternoon at the swimming hole, while he was crouched in the shadows across from the Bennett house. He was also still feeling the anger and shame he felt after learning that Elizabeth had lied to him, and used him. He almost would have preferred to ride out there and find an ambush.

He knew Sally was home, because he had gotten close enough to the house to look in the window. He saw Sally, and her mother, but not Clyde. Wherever he was, Clint hoped he wouldn't come home at the wrong time and get in the way.

As his stomach started to growl he was wishing he had gotten something to eat before coming over. The two women were probably having dinner while he crouched out there. How dumb was he not to even have brought a piece of beef jerky with him?

Finally, it looked like the lights were being extinguished in the house. If Sally was sneaking out tonight she was apparently waiting for her mother to turn in.

On the other hand, as all the lights went out, maybe she wasn't going to sneak out tonight. Maybe she and her mother both went to bed for the night, and Clint was sitting in the dark for no reason.

Then he saw something.

Movement.

There was enough moonlight—and his eyes were well used to the conditions—that he was able to see Sally Bennett climbing out a window. He wondered why, with the house dark, indicating that her mother had turned in, Sally didn't just come out the front door. But that wasn't important. What was important was that Sally did leave the house, and she had a sack slung over her shoulder.

Skinner had said that, on the previous night, Sally ran from the house and he lost her. But now she simply slunk away from the house, possibly because of the weight of the sack.

Clint stood, his knees creaking, and started after her. He skirted the house, and went into the trees, keeping Sally within sight. Hopefully this was it and she would lead him to Ted Horton. If she didn't he wasn't sure he would stay in Carthage past this night. The Hortons were a family he didn't have much liking for, except possibly for Tom—and even he was simply doing what his father had told him to do.

On the other hand, Clint had the feeling something else was going on here, and he wasn't sure his blasted curiosity would let him leave without finding out just what it was.

So he followed.

# Chapter Forty-One

They went on in the dark for a mile or two. She obviously knew the way, didn't trip once over a stray rock or root. Clint did not have the same luck. He stumbled several times, once almost pitched forward onto his face. But he managed to retain his feet and continue to follow without tipping her off.

Finally, she led him to a mine. He knew there were a lot of mines around Carthage, yielding all different types of ore. This one, apparently, had been tapped out, and the entrance looked to be boarded up.

In the moonlight he could see her approach the front, move a board aside, and climb through. He then broke from cover and approached. He was able to move aside the loose board and go inside without making much noise.

Once inside, letting the board slide back behind him, he was suddenly in total darkness. Ahead of him, he could hear the drone of voices. He waited a few moments until his eyes had readjusted to the darkness, and then started forward, shuffling his feet for safety purposes.

The voices got louder and, suddenly he could see a light ahead of him.

He continued forward, even slower, until he came to the end of the tunnel. He stopped and saw Sally crouching down next to a man who was seated on a cot.

" . . . so hungry," he was saying.

"I took what I could from the kitchen, hopin' Ma won't notice. Here's a couple of pieces of cold chicken."

"And somethin' to drink?"

"A canteen with water," Sally said.

He grabbed it and drank from it, then bit into a fat chicken leg. Clint could make out his face and knew that this was the missing Ted Horton. He could also see that Ted was plainly the better looking of the 3 brothers. There was enough of a resemblance, but he clearly had many of his mother's attributes.

He had two options: leave the way he came and go to Cyrus Horton with the news that he found his son, or step out now and find out what the hell had been going on.

He stepped out.

"Take it easy, you two," he said.

Sally jumped to her feet and turned to face him. Behind her, Ted looked at him, wide-eyed, but didn't get to his feet to run. He just sat and continued to eat his chicken leg.

"What are you doin' here?" the girl demanded. "You can't be here."

"Like I said, take it easy," Clint said. "I want to talk to you—both of you."

"Who are you?" Ted asked.

"My name's Clint Adams. Your father asked me to help find you. He thinks you've been kidnapped."

"No he don't," Ted said.

"He knows Ted left on his own," Sally said.

"Did he?" Clint asked. "Or did he leave because of you?"

"Me?" She looked puzzled. "Why would he leave because of me?"

"Well . . . he's hiding here and you're bringing him food," Clint said. "Aren't the two of you running away together. Aren't you . . . in love?"

"In love?" Suddenly, Sally covered her mouth with her hands. Clint thought she might be crying, but then he heard her giggling.

"What makes you think we're runnin' away together?" Ted asked. "She's just a kid."

"I'm seventeen!" Sally said.

"Well," Ted said to her, "I'm a lot older."

"Then, Ted, what are you doing here?" Clint looked around. Other than the cot, there was nothing else in the mine anybody could use. No table, no chairs, nothing.

"I'm here to get away from my father," Ted said.

"And I'm helpin' him."

"Why?" Clint asked.

"Because we got somethin' in common," Sally said. "I wanna get away from my father, too."

"No," Clint said, "I was talking to Ted. Why do you want to get away from your father?" He looked at the young man.

"He's not a good man," Ted said. "He's not a nice man, and he's not a good father. Do I need any other reasons?"

"What about your brothers? Your sister?"

"They got their own lives," Ted said. "They're gonna leave, eventually."

"Ted . . . I've heard different things about you."

"Yeah," Sally said, "I bet you heard he's simple. He ain't."

"And what's your part in this if you're not running away together, Sally?" Clint asked.

"I'm just helpin' him," Sally said. "We're friends."

"That's right," Ted said. "We're friends."

"Well, how long do you intend to stay in here?" Clint asked.

"Until I figure out my next move," Ted said.

Clint saw there was plenty of room on Ted's cot.

"Do you mind if I sit?" he asked.

"No," Ted said, "go ahead."

He sat on the other end of it, leaving room between them for Sally, if she chose to join them.

"You wouldn't happen to have some whiskey on you, would ya?" Ted asked. He jerked his head toward Sally. "She never brings any."

"You don't need no whiskey!" Sally scolded him.

"Sally, thanks for the food, water and supplies," Ted said. "Don't you think you better get home before your mother notices you're gone?"

"And leave you here with him?" she asked. Then she lowered her voice, as if Clint couldn't hear her. "Your father sent him."

Ted whispered back, "I think I'll be all right."

Sally looked at Clint. "You better not hurt him."

"Last thing on my mind," he replied.

She started to leave.

"Will you be okay on your own?" Clint asked.

"I'll be fine," she said. "You just watch your step goin' back. You might trip and break your leg."

She went into the tunnel and they could hear her rushing to the front.

"Now what?" Ted asked.

## Chapter Forty-Two

"I don't know," Clint said. "Your father asked me to find you, and I have. But he thought you had either wandered off in a daze or been kidnapped. He won't accept that you left on your own."

"I know that," Ted said. "It would never occur to him that any of us want to leave his house."

"Why didn't you take your horse?"

"Well," Ted said, "once he got it through his head that I did leave on my own, he'd never accept that I took a horse."

"But it's your horse, isn't it?"

"Oh no," Ted said, "everything belongs to my father."

"Ted . . . what's this simple minded stuff?"

"Oh, that," he said. "Well, I did have an accident as a kid and I did hit my head. But I survived. And I have had some—what did the doctor call them—episodes over the years after that. Those stopped a while ago—but I'm the only one who knows it."

"So you've been faking being simple minded?"

"From time-to-time," Ted said.

"And nobody knows it?"

"Well . . . maybe Lisa had an idea."

"But your sister kept your secret?"

"Of course," Ted said. "But she does have her own plans."

"So why don't you and Lisa leave together?" Clint asked.

"We're not that close," Ted said. "We're not gonna travel together."

"So you walked off a couple of days ago, and you've been in this mine ever since?"

"Pretty much."

"How did you get Sally to help you?"

"Sally's a good kid, and I think she has a crush on me. But like we said, we're just friends. She agreed to help me."

He took out another piece of chicken and drank some more water.

Clint watched him. He had been looking into the man's eyes while he was talking, looking for some sign that he might not be in his right mind. It might be said that a man who preferred to crouch in a mine rather than live in a huge house wasn't in his right mind.

"Mr. Adams, I don't suppose you'd consider bring' me a bottle of whiskey at some point."

"At some point?" Clint asked. "How much longer do you intend to be here?"

"What's wrong with here?" Ted asked, spreading his hands. "It's not so bad."

Clint looked around. It was worse than bad, it was awful.

"Ted," Clint said, "maybe you should let me take you home."

Ted was biting into another chicken leg when Clint said that. Now he stopped and turned his head.

"Why the hell would I go back?" he demanded. "My father's got a new wife, he's gonna leave the entire business to Tom, and he made Tim the sheriff."

"Why would he leave you the business, or make you sheriff, when you pretend to be simple minded."

Ted stared at Clint, and after a few minutes Clint wondered if the man had gone into a trance.

"Ted?"

No answer. And then Ted went back to his chicken.

"Okay," Clint said. He was starting to believe some of the things he had heard. Ted just might have spells making his mind wander, or he wasn't thinking straight. He didn't think he could just leave the man there. Once he left, what was there to keep Ted where he was? He could go and find another hiding place. The only way Clint was going to convince Cyrus that Ted had left on his own was to bring him back.

"Ted," He said, "I think it's time to go."

Ted looked at him and smiled.

"Where are we goin'?" he asked. "Will I have a good time?"

"I don't know if you'll have a good time," he said, grabbing Ted's arm and hauling him to his feet, "but you'll have a better time than you're having here."

He guided Ted along the tunnel to the front of the mine. He pulled the broken board aside for Ted to go through.

That's when the shots came.

# Chapter Forty-Three

"Get back!" Clint shouted, pulling Ted back.

Ted staggered back, fell onto his butt, and looked up at Clint, still with a chicken leg between his teeth.

He took the chicken leg out, said, "Boom," and then put it back.

There was no longer any doubt. Ted was addled. Also, somebody was keeping him in that mine and didn't want to let him out. A ransom note was probably imminent, if Cyrus had not already received it.

"Hey Adams," a voice called, "come on out. Leave ol' Teddy in there, though. We don't want some hunk of flyin' lead to find him." The speaker cackled a high pitched laugh. Clint thought he recognized the voice but couldn't be sure.

"Who's that out there?" he shouted.

"It's your old friend, Jimmy Gates."

Gates! The young man in the saloon who Bennett was supposed to have been drinking with.

"Gates, what're you doing here?" Clint asked.

"That's my boy you got in there, Adams," Gates said. "We can't let him go. Not just yet, anyway. We're still tryin' to figure out how much money we can get from his Pa for him."

"Turns out," Clint said, "less and less the longer you keep him."

That was met by silence.

He wondered if Sally was out there or if she had gone home.

"Is Sally still out there?"

"I let'er go home," Gates said. He laughed again. "She told me how you thought her and Teddy was together. That's funny. See, Sally's my gal."

"Isn't she a little young for you?"

"She's older than her years in lots of ways, Adams," Gates said. "She knows a lot more than most seventeen year olds. Fact is, she learned a lot of it at Miss Buffet's nickel-a-poke house."

That was more than Clint wanted to know about the young girl.

"Gates, are you alone?"

"Well, sure I'm alone," Gates called back. "I had a shootout with a friend of mine over you, and I won. I get to kill you, but I didn't think it would be like this."

Clint felt that Gates had slipped up and said "we" a couple of times, which led him to believe he was not out there alone, but with his buddies. They wanted him to step out so they could gun him down.

He looked at Ted, who seemed to be concentrating on something he found interesting on the ground.

"Ted, is there another way out of here?"

No answer.

He got down on a knee in front of the man, hoping to draw him back from whatever dark recesses of his mind he had retreated to.

Taking Ted by his shoulders, he shook him and said, "Is there another way out of here?"

Ted looked at him, his eyes focused for a moment, and he pointed behind them.

"Show me."

"Adams," Gates called, "you got five minutes to come out and leave Ted behind. Oh, and bring your gun!"

"Come on," Clint said, pulling Ted to his feet. He grabbed the chicken bone from his hand and tossed it away. "Show me!" he said, again.

"This way," Ted said, and started back up the tunnel.

When they reached the cavern they had been sitting in, Ted kept walking and chose another tunnel branching off from it. If Jimmy Gates was still shouting, Clint could no longer hear him. Hopefully, whatever exit Ted was taking him to was unknown to Jimmy and his partners; hopefully, Ted knew where he was going.

"Ted, how do you know there's a way out of here?" Clint asked.

"My Pa owns this mine," Ted said, "and I ain't had that much to do these past few days except explore it."

So Clint kept following and they kept going deeper and deeper into the mountain. Eventually, Clint started to feel a breeze on his face.

And then there was moonlight ahead.

"There it is," Ted said, pointing. "You go on ahead, and I'll just go back—"

"Whoa," Clint said, grabbing the back of Ted's shirt to keep him from going back into the tunnel. "You're comin' with me."

"Where we goin'?" Ted asked.

"You'll see," Clint said, slapping him on the back "You're going to like it."

"Oh, good."

Walking behind Ted, Clint noticed how dirty his expensive clothes were.

Outside Clint tried to get his bearings, but finally he turned to Ted and asked, "Which way is town?" hoping he would be right minded enough to know.

# Chapter Forty-Four

They got back to town without encountering Jimmy Gates and his men. Clint was tempted to go to the Bennett house and expose Sally, but decided that could wait. Instead, they went to the livery stable and woke the hostler who was sleeping in the back.

"I need a horse for my friend," Clint said.

"Hey," the man said, squinting, "ain't he—"

"Never mind who he is," Clint said. "Just rent me a horse."

Clint saddled Eclipse and the rented horse, and then they left and headed for the Horton house.

***

Clint was glad it was dark, and nobody saw him riding out of town with Ted Horton. There would have been a passel of people claiming they found him.

They rode slowly because of the darkness, but eventually there was a light ahead, and then he saw the house with a light downstairs and a light upstairs.

"Hey," Ted said, "that's my daddy's house."

"Yeah, it is."

Ted yanked on his horse's reins, stopping the animal short.

"I don't wanna go there!"

"That's too bad," Clint said. "I'm hoping it's for your own good."

"Livin' in that house ain't for nobody's good," Ted said, completely lucid at the moment.

"Come on," Clint said, and slapped Ted's horse on the rump.

\*\*\*

They rode to the front of the house where Clint dismounted, and then had to drag Ted off his horse.

"No!" Ted shouted.

"Yes," Clint replied, and pushed him up the steps.

He knocked on the door, which was answered by Elizabeth.

"Clint—"

Clint cut her off by shoving Ted through the doorway. Elizabeth staggered back.

"Where's your husband?"

"In his office, but—"

"That's her!" Ted said, pointing.

"Who?"

"My father's new wife! That's her!"

"Yes, it is," Clint said, "but we're not here to see her. We're here to see your father."

"Pa," Ted said, then he turned and headed for his father's office, shouting, "Pa, I'm home!"

Clint followed, with Elizabeth close behind.

Cyrus came out of his office, saw Ted and started toward him. They came together in the center of the hallway.

"Pa!" Ted said.

Cyrus backhanded his son across the face, then took him in his arms and hugged him.

"And that," Elizabeth said from behind Clint, "is my husband in a nutshell."

Cyrus looked at Clint over Ted's shoulder.

"Thank you, Adams. I'll see you're paid handsomely."

"Do you want to know where he was?" Clint asked. "And why?"

"I'm just glad he's back," Cyrus said. "Elizabeth will put you together with Hardesty. You can give him all the details."

Cyrus turned and walked back to the office, drew Ted inside with him, and closed the door.

Clint turned to Elizabeth.

"I don't want to talk to Hardesty," he said. "I want to talk to Tom."

"Fine."

"And to Tim and Eloise."

"What for?"

He leaned in and said, "Because they're family."

\*\*\*

He spoke to Tom first, then had Tom get ahold of Tim and Eloise. They all met in Clint's hotel room.

"What's goin' on?" Eloise asked.

"Yeah, why are we here?" Sheriff Tim asked.

"I found Ted," Clint said.

"Where is he?" Tom asked.

"I took him home. He's with your father."

"No," Eloise said, "why couldn't you leave him alone?"

"I couldn't do that, Lisa," Clint said. "He's not in his right mind. He's been hiding in a mine all this time—only he was being held there."

"By who?" Tim asked.

"You know Jimmy Gates?"

"I know 'im."

"He and his partners," Clint said. "They got ahold of Ted with the help of Sally Bennett. Ted thought she was his friend."

"How'd you get 'im out?" Tom asked.

"They had the front entrance covered," Clint said. "Ted knew another way out."

"Not in his right mind?" Eloise asked, as if she hadn't heard any of the other conversation.

"No," Clint said, "he needs help."

"From Pa?" Eloise asked.

"From you," Clint said. "His brothers and his sister."

"What are we supposed to do?" Tom asked.

"Pay closer attention to him," Clint said. "I can't tell you exactly what to do. But you're going to have to come together as a family and watch him."

The three Horton siblings looked at each other.

"I wanna get out," Eloise said.

"Stay, Lisa," Tom said. "We need you."

Eloise and Tom looked at Tim.

"I'll be around," Tim said. "I just took a new job. Seems Chief Collins sent those idiots into the saloon the other night and liked the way I handled it. I'm a Carthage police officer now."

"That's good," Clint said. "The three of you can make sure your brother is treated right and never wanders off."

"But he didn't wander off," Tom said. "He was lured away by Sally Bennett. That's what you said."

"Sally was under the influence of Jimmy Gates."

"And where is Gates now?" Tim asked. "I might as well start doin' my job."

"He's around somewhere," Clint said. "But I believe I'll be seeing him in the morning, before I leave town."

"You're leaving tomorrow?" Eloise asked.

"That's right," Clint said. "I think I've been in Carthage long enough."

"My father wants to pay you," Tom said.

"Tell him to keep it," Clint replied.

"Now we only have to deal with that bitch, Elizabeth," Tom said.

"Don't worry about that, dear brother," Eloise said. "I believe she's on the next train to St. Louis."

"Well . . . how do we thank you?" Tom asked, turning to Clint.

"There's no need," Clint said. "As long as you're all together when I ride out, that's thanks enough."

"And you think we'll stay that way?" Eloise asked.

"For a while . . ." Clint said.

# Chapter Forty-Five

It was late, but once the Hortons left, Clint was still able to get a steak in the hotel diningroom. He was eating it at a leisurely pace when Chief Collins entered the room and approached his table.

"I heard you've got a new man," Clint said.

"Seems like he wasn't happy as sheriff," Collins said. "I think he'll be happier now and a better man. You mind if I sit?"

"Not at all. You want something?"

"If you mean food, I ate," Collins said.

"What else is there?"

"I heard you brought Ted Horton back home."

"That's right, I did," Clint said. "His family is rallying around him tonight."

"Well, good for him. But I also heard you know who was holding him."

"If you heard that from Tim, then you know who?"

"Jimmy Gates."

"Right."

"Tim says you're going to take care of Gates yourself," Collins said. "I'd rather you didn't do that."

"The choice isn't mine," Clint said.

"How do you mean?"

"Gates said he had a shootout with a friend of his to see who was going to kill me. He won."

"But you took Ted home," Collins said. "It's over."

"That part of it is over," Clint said. "I don't think the wanting to kill me part is."

"So what are you going to do?"

"Well," Clint said, "my plan was to ride out in the morning."

"Was?"

"Yes," Clint said, "if I do that, they might ambush me on the trail."

"I see."

"So I just thought I'd give them the opportunity to end it right here in town."

"That's what I'm trying to avoid."

"Me, too." He put the last hunk of steak into his mouth.

"But you just said—"

"If I'm right," Clint said, "they'll be waiting for me when I leave the hotel in the morning. Now, I'll give them the opportunity to walk away, so it'll be up to them what happens after that."

Collins sat back and stared at him.

"I could arrest them."

"On what charge?"

"I'll make one up."

"And then you'll have to let them out," Clint said. "And if a judge realized what you did, you'll be in trouble."

"But I will have kept my streets from being shot up."

Clint put down his silverware and sat back.

"What if I can get them to meet me outside of town?" Clint asked. "Then it doesn't happen in your streets."

"Somebody's still going to get killed though," Collins said.

"More than likely."

Collins rubbed his right hand over his face.

"I shouldn't even be hearing this."

"Look," Clint suggested, "put a couple of your men outside the hotel—you know, in their uniforms. That might scare them away."

"I can do that."

"Then once I ride out," Clint said, "you can stop thinking about it."

"What about that ambush?"

"I'll keep my eyes open, Chief," Clint said. "I promise."

# Chapter Forty-Six

Clint came down the next morning, paid his bill and then walked to the front window. He saw two of Collins' uniformed police across the street, watching the hotel. Neither of them was Tim Horton. There was no sign of Jimmy Gates.

When he stepped out the front door the two uniformed men came to attention and watched. Clint stopped just outside the door and looked both ways on the street. There was no sign of Jimmy Gates and his friends. He turned and started walking to the livery stable.

He doubted Gates and his partners were still waiting outside the mine. They must have discovered by now that Clint and Ted had gotten out. And they must have heard that Ted Horton was home. As Clint passed people on the street, he heard them talking about it. The whole town knew.

He turned to look behind him. The two policemen were not following him to the livery. He didn't think they would. Their orders were to watch the front of the hotel.

When he reached the stable he stopped across the street and had a look, then crossed over and entered. The hostler was nowhere to be found so he went and saddled Eclipse. That done, he knew he would have to find the man to settle his bill, but he had a feeling that would come later.

"Gettin' ready to leave town, Adams?"

He turned and saw Jimmy Gates standing between him and the door.

"Hello, Jimmy."

"Pretty slick gettin' Ted outta that mine. But that's okay, we'll just have to grab him again."

"I think you'll find it a bit harder next time, Jimmy," Clint said. "If there is a next time."

"And why wouldn't there be?"

"Because I get the feeling you're about to make a very bad—and fatal—mistake."

"No," Gates said, "you made the mistake."

Now another man came from his right, and a second from his left. Clint was facing 3 men.

"See?" Gates said. "I've decided to play it safe. Three against one."

"Only one problem," Clint said.

"What's that?"

"You're still outnumbered."

Gates laughed and looked around.

"You still look alone to me," he said.

"That's what I mean," Clint said. "You're outnumbered and outgunned."

Gates and his two partners all went for their guns.

None of them cleared leather.

As the 3 men fell to the ground dead, the hostler came from the back and said to Clint, "You wanna settle yer bill, Mr. Adams?"

"I do." Clint ejected the spent shells, reloaded and holstered his gun.

"How much do I owe you?" he asked.

"Uh," the man said, "I think I'm gonna make this on the house."

Coming October 27, 2018

# THE GUNSMITH
## 441
## Aces & Queens

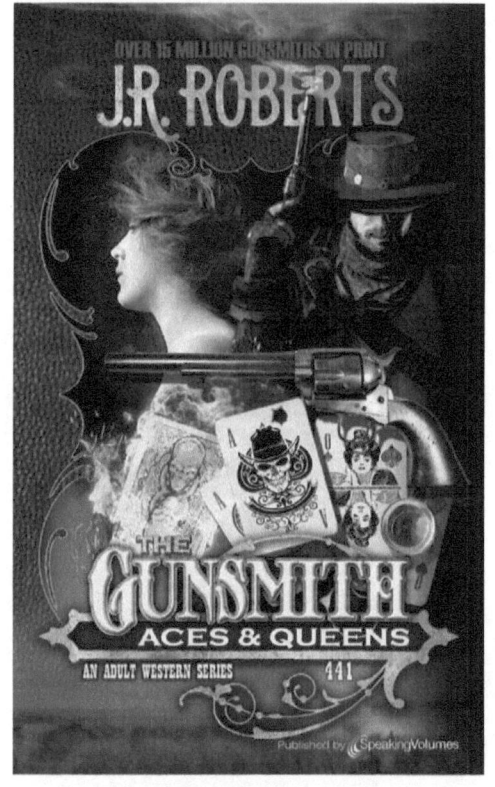

**For more information
visit:** www.speakingvolumes.us

# On Sale Now!

## THE GUNSMITH
### 439

## For more information
### visit: www.speakingvolumes.us

# On Sale Now!

## THE GUNSMITH
### 438

**For more information
visit:** www.speakingvolumes.us

# On Sale Now!

## THE GUNSMITH
### 437

**For more information
visit:**

# On Sale Now!

## THE GUNSMITH
### 435

## For more information
visit: www.speakingvolumes.us

# On Sale Now!

## THE GUNSMITH
### 434

## For more information
visit: www.speakingvolumes.us

# On Sale Now!

## THE GUNSMITH
### 433

## For more information
visit: www.speakingvolumes.us

# On Sale Now!

## THE GUNSMITH
### 432

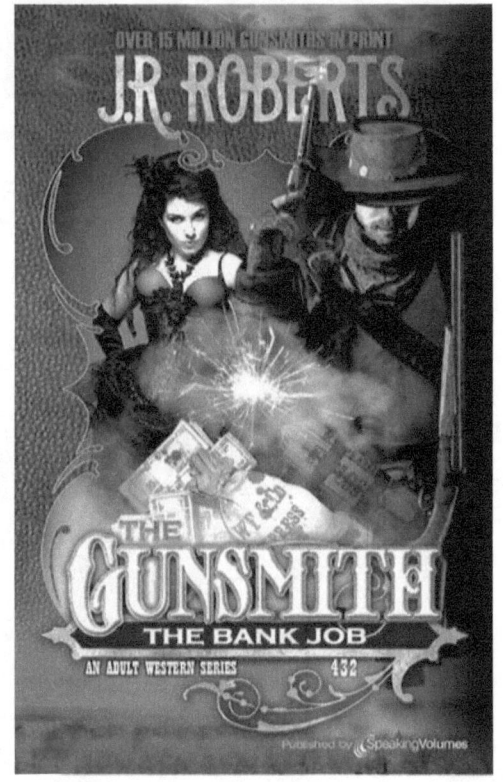

# On Sale Now!

## THE GUNSMITH
### 430

## For more information
visit: www.speakingvolumes.us

# On Sale Now!

**TRACKER** *series*
**by**
**Award-Winning Author**
**Robert J. Randisi (J.R. Roberts)**

## For more information
**visit:**